ROBOT

There was the crackle of static electricity and a fluttering sound. Within the machine flowed [illegible] *life*!

The robot lifted his [illegible] crate which splintered [illegible] rose to his feet, stretch[illegible] hand of the boy besid[illegible] low, steady voice.

'Who are you?' sai[illegible] shining eyes.

'I am Drumnadrockit,' said the robot.

Also by Peter Grimwade:

Doctor Who – Time-Flight
Doctor Who – Mawdryn Undead
Doctor Who – Planet of Fire

ROBOT

Peter Grimwade

A STAR BOOK
published by
the Paperback Division of
W.H. ALLEN & Co. PLC

A Star Book
Published in 1987
by the Paperback Division of
W.H. Allen & Co. Plc
44 Hill Street, London W1X 8LB

**Printed and bound in Great Britain by
Anchor Brendon Ltd, Tiptree, Essex**

ISBN 0 352 32036 2

PROLOGUE

It was the end.

A forlorn assembly of some twenty men and women stood silently waiting in the control bunker, like mourners at a funeral. Which is exactly what they were. The view on the scanner screens showed the object of their grief: a dead planet. The fatherland was now no more than a cinder floating in space, its fields an arid wilderness, its atmosphere a poisonous smog. Twelve million years of civilisation had been destroyed and an entire race annihilated - except, that is, for the unhappy few who lingered in the underground command centre. Such were the fortunes of war.

The President turned to his Supreme Commander. 'Is all prepared?'

'The destruct mechanism is primed. We are waiting for your final command, Mister President,' replied a uniformed officer standing beside one of the systems units.

An older man in a severe black robe now entered the chamber from another room. He was followed by several assistants, younger, but in similarly sombre dress. The last of the newcomers, a young woman, carried a silver disc some ten inches in diameter.

'Well, Moderator?' the President addressed the old man.

'The data is compiled,' announced the Moderator. He turned to the woman attendant and took from her hands the shining disc, holding it up for all to see. 'The token of our planet. All that was, and is, and shall be of Vardon.'

The assistant crossed to a panel in the corner of the chamber and opened a small hatch to reveal a sphere nestling inside the recessed cavity. She lifted out the sphere and offered it to the Moderator. The old man guided the disc to a narrow aperture in the side of the sphere which closed as soon as the silver wafer had been absorbed. The sphere - which now contained the disc - was placed, once more, in the cavity and the door sealed.

The Moderator raised his arm in a ritual gesture. Hail and farewell. There was a dull thud from the direction of the, now empty, compartment. The sphere and its precious contents were launched on a vast journey through space.

'Let us hope,' said the President, 'that the people of Earth will, one day, learn from our mistakes.'

The Supreme Commander stepped forward to activate the machinery that would bring to an end their distress. 'Mister President. Are you ready?'

But the President was still thinking of a small insignificant planet in a far-distant corner of the Galaxy. 'Tell me,' said the Leader of the Vardons, turning to the man in black. 'What is the name of the Earth Child you have chosen?'

'His name,' said the Moderator gravely, 'is Tolemy.'

CHAPTER ONE

'I'm called Tolemy!' said Tolemy, smiling at the solicitor across the huge, cluttered desk.

'I'm fully aware of that,' replied Mr Mowbray somewhat testily. 'Otherwise I would not have asked you to come and see me.' He looked down at his blotter and shuffled through some papers, distracted by the self-confidence of the boy who faced him in the upright chair.

Tolemy turned and grinned at his father who was perched, stiff and Sunday-suited, on the broken springs of Mr Mowbray's sofa. Looking far more at home in his jeans and T shirt than his father did in his suit, Tolemy proceeded to examine the room. It was dirty and dusty, cluttered with papers and old books. The furniture was ugly and old-fashioned. The carpet had a hole in it and he could count at least six unwashed coffee cups, their saucers brimming with wet cigarette ends. The letter that had arrived for him at home a week before had led Tolemy to expect something far grander.

Barton, Barton & Mowbray (Solicitors),
18b, The Precinct,
Turlow New Town.

Dear Tolemy James,
Concerning the last will and testament of my client, the late Charles Protheroe. If you would arrange to visit my office at your earliest convenience, you will learn something to your advantage.
Yours sincerely,
K.W. MOWBRAY

Of course, Tolemy's dad had said it was all a mistake, seeing how they'd never ever heard of a Mr Protheroe. But Tolemy's mother thought it would be rude not to go and see what sort of advantage Mr Mowbray had in mind.

Which is how, on the first day of the school holidays, Tolemy and his father caught the bus into town and found their way to the narrow door between Monsieur Cassidy's Hair Salon and the Chinese takeaway. Sitting in the dingy, first floor office, they now waited for the mystery to be explained.

'As I said,' said Mr Mowbray loftily, 'a considerable portion of the Protheroe estate is bequeathed to one Tolemy James of 3, Beachcroft Close, Turlow New Town...'

'That's me,' repeated Tolemy.

'Precisely,' muttered the solicitor, uncomfortably aware that the contents of a Rotary lunch were beginning to rumble in his stomach like a Bakerloo Line train. Mr Mowbray got up from his desk and walked over to the window. He burped gently and started, absent-mindedly, to scratch his behind.

'Been a bit of a mix-up if you ask me,' said Tolemy's dad politely, from the direction of the sofa.

'Indeed?' Mr Mowbray turned from the window, fishing a packet of Park Drive from his jacket pocket.

'The boy doesn't know any Charles Protheroe. None of us do.'

'That is neither here nor there,' observed the solicitor, returning to his desk. 'The point is, my client knew your son.'

Terry James looked doubtfully in Tolemy's direction, wishing now that he'd stayed at home and fitted the new CB radio in the cab of his lorry.

'Are you telling me this bloke's left me something in his will?' said Tolemy, watching Mowbray's yellow fingers claw at a cigarette lighter.

'Quite so,' replied the solicitor, drawing on the cigarette.

'How much?'

Mr Mowbray was suddenly convulsed with a violent fit of coughing. As Tolemy waited patiently for the hacking and the gasping to subside he began to yawn. Lately he hadn't been getting much sleep. A recurring nightmare had been disturbing his nights.

Mr Mowbray blew his nose on a rather grey handkerchief.

'How much?' repeated Tolemy, wondering what it would feel like being a millionaire.

'It's hardly a question of money,' said Mr Mowbray reprovingly. 'Quite the opposite, in fact.'

'Never mind, eh?' Tolemy grinned philosophically.

'More of a white elephant if you ask me.'

'You what?'

Mr Mowbray drew out some documents from a folder. 'My client was the owner of a property on the edge of the Old Town. Down by the canal. 68, Droop Street, to be precise.'

'It's all industrial, down by the canal,' interrupted Terry James.

'That's right, Mr James. Your son is now the proud proprietor of Tinkerbell Toys.'

'The old doll factory?'

'Complete with good will and all appertinences, fixtures and fittings.'

'What does our Tolemy want with a doll factory!' protested Mr James.

'Not a lot,' agreed the solicitor gloomily. 'It's in a shocking state of repair. Losing money like one o'clock. Charlie only kept it going because he couldn't afford the redundancy payments.'

'Well, I don't know,' said Mr James doubtfully. 'Do you, Tolemy?'

Tolemy said nothing. He was busy studying the plans of his property. The drawing looked strangely familiar. But that was impossible. He'd never been to Tinkerbell Toys in his life. Unless it was in one of those dreams...

'How old are you, Tolemy?'

'Fifteen last June,' his father answered for him.

'You realise, Mr James, that until Tolemy comes of age, you will be responsible for the lad's inheritance.'

'Well, I don't know,' said Tolemy's dad, once more.

'Look on the bright side, Mr James. You might end up making quite a go of it.' Mr Mowbray puffed expansively at another cigarette.

'Are you sure this is all on the level?'

'I beg your pardon?'

'Like, legal.'

'I should damn well hope so,' said the solicitor. 'Of course there'll be probate, death duties, my own small fee...'

'I mean, this guy Protheroe and Tolemy. They were complete strangers!'

'Not to worry, Mr James. My client must have spotted your boy somewhere. Taken a fancy to him. Who can tell? Old Charlie Protheroe was nothing if not eccentric.' Mr Mowbray got slowly to his feet. 'Well, young man.' He turned to Tolemy who was lost in a dream of 68, Droop Street. 'Good luck!'

Tolemy jumped up and held out his hand. 'Thank you very much, Mr Mowbray.'

'Come on, Tolemy,' said Terry James, anxious to get out into the fresh air.

'Now there's a name to conjure with,' said Mr Mowbray, as they left. 'Egyptian, isn't it? *Tolemy*!'

'The tests will take place next Tuesday. The old tank testing ground on Turlow Heath.' General Spiby sat back in his chair and smiled victoriously at Field Marshal Montgomery. The Hero of El Alamein smiled stiffly back at his former subaltern from a large signed photograph on the wall of the Whitehall office. Once again the military men had stolen a march on their enemies in the Civil Service. 'We'll show them, by God!' exploded the old soldier, his sudden energy lighting up the room like a parachute flare.

'I wouldn't be too sure,' murmured his visitor, a bland, pale man with thinning hair and eyes watering from a painful experiment with contact lenses. Henry Fraddon stood with his back to the general, admiring the view of a Victorian tenement block whose fire escapes and dustbins were all that could be seen from the office window. The civil servant turned back to the general, dabbing his eyes with a handkerchief. He blinked at the strip lighting, which, in the perpetual winter of the hated Annex, blazed at maximum wattage all year round. 'Operation PZ1 has already gone massively over budget.'

The general scowled.

'My dear Arthur, we do have to think of the taxpayers' money.' Fraddon smiled sadly. 'It may even be necessary to close the entire Special Projects Department down.'

Big Ben tolled slowly in the distance as the two men stared at each other.

'Over my dead body!'

Henry Fraddon considered the prospect of General Spiby's demise with remarkable equanimity. In fact, he'd been wanting to get rid of the old boy along with the entire unit for years. Now, if the PZ1 Operation was a really spectacular failure they'd have a perfect excuse to close the whole thing down and hand the squalid Annex back to Auxiliary Typists from the DoE. But it would do his cause no good to be seen publicly molesting Spiby's brain child. 'I understand the Minister wants to bring along some American observers, as well as our European friends.' He adroitly changed the subject.

'Americans?'

'The technology could be useful in their Strategic Defence Initiative.'

'Star Wars!' The general snorted derisively.

'This sort of robotic development is cripplingly expensive. If we can offload some of the research costs . . .

'Listen, Fraddon. I'm not interested in playing space invaders. The danger's here on Earth. In our own country. Civil war!'

'Oh, really, Arthur,' protested Henry Fraddon, who had seen little evidence of civil war in his native Wimbledon.

'Toxteth, Brixton, Birmingham. We face a complete breakdown of law and order.'

'I'm sure the Home Office has the matter in hand.'

'Water cannon and plastic bullets are all very well. But to maintain ultimate *control* we need an entirely new *force*!'

As Fraddon waited patiently for the general to ride out his hobby horse he noticed the pencil clutched in Spiby's right hand which had started to move, like the glass on a ouija board, across the back of a departmental memo.

Fraddon peered forward to get a better view of the general's automatic writing.

'We'll soon deal with the terrorists and the muggers, and all those pickets and commies and queers,' lectured General Spiby, unaware of the sudden independence of his own right hand. 'An iron fist in an iron glove...'

He broke off, aware that Fraddon was staring at the paper on his desk. The general looked down at the document on which he had been scribbling absent-mindedly. He had drawn a face. Hard and angular, with glaring eyes and a cruel rapacious mouth. Embarrassed at this manifestation of his subconscious, General Spiby quickly screwed up the paper and threw it in the waste paper basket.

'I must be getting back to my own office,' said Henry Fraddon discreetly.

'Yes, of course,' muttered the general.

The intercom buzzed. 'Excuse me, General...'

'Yes, Miss Wheeler?'

'There's a Mr Hastie at reception.'

'Hastie? Hastie? Rings a bell.'

'He's been writing to you. Something about tanks...'

'Tanks!' purred the general, and actually began to smile.

As Henry Fraddon hurried down the lavatorial corridor that connected the Annex with the Main Building, a rather mousey-looking man of about 55 emerged from the lift. 'I'm looking for General Spiby,' he said.

Fraddon quickly checked the pass pinned on the lapel of the visitor's shiny blue blazer and directed him back down the passage towards the general's door.

'Captain Hastie!' The general held out a hand to his guest. 'Come and take a pew.'

'Good of you to see me at last,' said Mr Hastie, depositing himself in a leather armchair.

'You're keeping fit, I see.'

'Mustn't grumble,' said Mr Hastie, wondering what sort of game the general was playing with him.

The general ran his eyes over Hastie's frayed turn-ups, his patched blazer and worn-out Hush Puppies and wondered if he should have a word with the secretary of the Veterans' Association. Perhaps they could organise something from the hardship fund. 'If it's about money,' said the general gruffly...

'It's about Turlow Heath,' said Mr Hastie.

The general frowned.

'Those disgusting tanks of yours.'

'I beg your pardon!' spluttered the general.

'You realise you're desecrating a Bronze Age burial ground?'

'I don't get your drift, Hastie.'

'Can't you go and play somewhere else with your nasty, dirty toys?'

General Spiby wondered if his hearing was defective. 'What sort of talk is this for an old Desert Rat!' he blustered.

'Beg pardon?' said Mr Hastie.

'North Africa. The old Tank Regiment.'

'You must be thinking of somebody else.'

'Dash it all. You said you were Paddy Hastie.'

'My name is Leslie,' said Mr Hastie.

'In that case, I don't want to see you.'

'You're already seeing me,' said his visitor, chuckling at the misunderstanding, which, after weeks of fruitless letter-writing to the Ministry, had brought him to see the Big White Chief himself.

'How dare you come in here, impersonating an officer?'

'I *was* an officer, actually,' protested Mr Hastie. 'National Service. I was a Captain in the Pay Corps.'

Apoplectic with rage, the general stared at the horrible, threadbare little man in front of him. He raised an accusing finger at the faded coat of arms on Mr Hastie's breast pocket. 'Before you leave this room you will remove that regimental badge from your blazer!'

'Got it wrong again, General.' Hastie's eyes twinkled. 'That is the crest of the Turlow Building Society of which I was deputy manager until my early retirement in June of last year.'

Rigid with fury, General Spiby seized a freshly sharpened pencil with his right hand.

'You see, I wanted to spend more time on my historical research.'

The general saw that his own right hand was unconsciously scribbling in the margin of his *Daily*

Telegraph. He quickly placed his left hand over the offending wrist. 'Get out!' he roared at the interloper.

But Leslie Hastie was made of sterner stuff, and was already unbuckling a battered, PVC attache case. 'I have here a petition from the Ley Hunters' Association of Turlow New Town. We demand full access and right of way to the hitherto restricted areas of Turlow Heath.' He leaned forward and deposited a bundle of papers on General Spiby's desk.

'Miss Wheeler,' snapped the general into his intercom. 'Ask Security to come up here, will you?'

Hastie realised his time was running out. 'Turlow Heath is an area of great cosmic importance. A unique alignment of the most powerful ley lines in England.'

Spiby snorted with unconcealed disdain. The man was not only an imposter but a crank into the bargain.

'Your tank testing ground is at the centre of a Great Decagon. A massive force field, set up in the Golden Age.'

A uniformed soldier entered the general's office.

'Ah, Sergeant Gunnel. Kindly escort this gentleman from the building.'

Leslie Hastie rose obediently to his feet. He'd had a pretty good run for his money. 'Thank you so much for seeing me, General. I'm sure you'll find our submissions most interesting.'

General Spiby picked up the documents that had been left on his desk and hurled them into the waste bin.

His parting visitor turned, undismayed, at the door. 'One word of warning. I suggest you keep your people well away from Tolemy's Tomb!'

Tolemy couldn't move. He couldn't hear. He couldn't see. He was buried alive. A lonely spark of light appeared somewhere in the darkness, bursting into a desert of white.

The Man in Black was sitting on a rock in front of him. 'Well, Tolemy,' said the old man. 'It's begun.'

'Who *are* you?' said Tolemy.

'I can't tell you that,' said the Man in Black. 'Because I don't exist. I'm a figment. A mere idea. But I shall be with you in the days to come. As I have been with you since the world began.'

The light grew brighter as the old man put on a suit of shining armour. *'Excelsior!'* the old man cried.

'Tolemy?'

Tolemy opened his eyes.

'Come on, sleeping beauty.' Tolemy's mum stood by the bedroom door.

Tolemy yawned. 'I was dreaming.'

'I'm off to work. Your breakfast's in the oven.'

Tolemy lay still, thinking about the dream. If only he could save the information like he could a program on the computer. But waking up was like clearing the system. However much he struggled to hold the fleeting memory, the data of each experience was erased by consciousness, until the next time. Where did it all come from? Perhaps he possessed in his brain his own RAM, a pre-programmed memory chip that could be accessed only in sleep.

Tolemy heaved himself out of bed, jumped into a pair of red briefs and pulled back the curtains. He peered out at the trim semis of the Beachcroft Estate. There were several brightly painted, regency front doors in the cul de sac, indicating those proud owners who had bought from the Council (with a little help from the Turlow Building Society). Tolemy remembered that he, too, was now a man of property. Tinkerbell Toys. But why had Charles Protheroe left the factory to an unknown teenager?

Curiously, he still felt no real surprise. His inheritance seemed to belong to the natural order of things. Like those extraordinary dreams . . .

The James house was as quiet as the grave as Tolemy ate his bacon and egg in the tiny kitchenette. His father had already left in the lorry for Southampton and his mother would be busy on the checkout at Woolworths until the evening. Tolemy poured himself another cup of luke-warm tea and studied the documents that Mr Mowbray, the solicitor, had given him. Some of the legal jargon was a bit beyond him. He'd have to get one of the Foxes to explain it to him.

Edwina Fox – or Eddie as she was known – was Tolemy's best friend. Eddie's father taught physics at Turlow Comprehensive and her mother worked part-time for

Citizens' Advice in the Precinct. The Foxes lived about ten minutes by bike from Beachcroft Close in a detached Victorian villa on the edge of the Old Town, hidden from the road by an enormous monkey puzzle tree.

Eddie had only just got up and was still in her dressing gown when Tolemy arrived at the front door of *Westaways*. 'Your mum and dad in?'

'Mum's on duty, and Bernard's gone to a teachers' conference at Milton Keynes. We've got the place to ourselves.'

Tolemy unfolded the plan of Tinkerbell Toys on the pine table in the Foxes' kitchen while Eddie started to grind coffee beans in one of Mrs Fox's numerous gadgets.

'Who wants a grotty old factory, anyway?' said Eddie, unimpressed, as the coffee gurgled and spluttered in a glass machine. 'Tell you what,' she suggested daringly. 'We could play my Pet Shop Boys cassettes on Bernard's hi-fi.'

Tolemy grinned. 'Why have you started calling your father *Bernard*?'

'He's got this thing about communication.'

'My dad would belt me if I called him Terry.'

'You're lucky.'

Tolemy returned to the plan of the old doll factory. 'They haven't drawn the corridor right,' he exclaimed. 'There should be a door here. And another room . . .'

'Thought you'd never been to Tinkerbell Toys?'

'It must have been the dream,' said Tolemy, trying desperately to remember his wanderings in the twilight world.

'Astral travelling,' explained Eddie Fox as they walked along the canal tow-path, between the Old Town gasworks and the New Town cemetery. 'I read about it in a novel. These people escaped in their sleep to the Ethereal Plane. Then they met the devil and the silver cord that keeps them in touch with their Earthly bodies got cut.'

'What happened next?'

'Bernard threw the book on the Aga.'

'Unscientific trash!' said Tolemy, imitating Mr Fox's schoolmaster's voice. He paused for a moment beside a rather dowdy gentleman who was sitting on a bollard, earnestly examining an ordnance survey map. The man fished in his knapsack and brought out a very professional-looking compass with which he proceeded to take a bearing on the distant tower of Saint Swithin's church.

'Oh, come on, Tolemy!' said Eddie, kicking at a plastic cola bottle. 'Let's go and have a drink at the Hoop.'

Tolemy looked shocked.

'I can easily pass for eighteen,' Eddie reassured him.

'My dad would skin *me* alive. Besides, I want to look at my factory.'

Mr Hastie put down his compass and turned to look at the disappearing boy. *'Tolemy?'* he repeated quietly to himself. 'How extraordinary!'

The two teenagers rounded the bend in the canal beside the abandoned dye works. Beyond the ruined, concrete hulk could be seen the slanted roofs and chimney of an equally gloomy but less decrepit industrial building.

'That's it,' said Tolemy confidently. 'Tinkerbell Toys.'

The factory consisted of a number of long workshops ranged in parallel like trains in a siding. Adjoining them was a blockhouse of hard, red brick, girded with metal ladders and walkways. To the side of the main building a large gasping flue pointed skywards like a space rocket. A small iron gate led from the tow-path of the canal to a loading bay inside the factory compound where a lorry was being filled with cardboard boxes.

Supervising the operation was a man in a woolly cardigan and baggy corduroy trousers who looked up as Eddie and Tolemy arrived at the gate. They realised, as he walked towards them, that he was quite a young man in spite of his middle-aged appearance.

'Hello,' said the man, 'I'm Bob Love. And you must be Mister Tolemy James.'

Tolemy! As he packed his gear into the haversack, Mr Hastie thought again about the boy he had just seen on the tow-path. The face was vaguely familiar – one of the kids from Beachcroft Close, he guessed. But the name. Could it be a coincidence? Or was the young man part of the chain!

CHAPTER TWO

Professor Melmo lay back in his deck chair, shaded by an apple tree from the morning sun, and listened to the buzzing of the bees as they guzzled forbidden pollen on the testing ground of nearby Turlow Heath.

The clattering from the kitchen had stopped. Mrs Erskine must have done the breakfast washing-up and be making herself a cup of tea. The swish of the scythe was no longer to be heard in the orchard, and in his mind's eye Professor Melmo could see Fred Erskine sitting on the upturned wheelbarrow, smoking his pipe and reading the *Sun*.

With a thump, Pythagoras landed in the Professor's lap. As he stroked the fat, purring, ginger tom, Professor Melmo became aware of a car approaching down the lane. A Fiesta, he guessed. There was the squeak of brakes, a single, muted slam; then, after a brief pause, he heard his own front doorbell ring twice. Allowing time for Mrs Erskine to let his unknown visitor in, Professor Melmo lowered Pythagoras to the grass and got up from his chair.

He opened the front door noiselessly and stood listening in the flagstoned hall. He heard Mrs Erskine calling him, as if he were a cat, from the open kitchen door at the rear of the cottage.

'Professor! Professor!'

The newcomer had apparently been shown into the tiny sitting room on his right. As he stood in the doorway the professor could hear the slight rustling of papers. One of the drawers of his bureau slid open... 'Good morning,' said the professor abruptly.

'Good morning, Professor.' Confident that he could not be seen, the visitor gently shut the open drawer and moved towards his host. 'Henry Fraddon. Special Projects Department.'

Professor Melmo held out his hand. 'I thought as much.'

The front door slammed and a breathless Mrs Erskine peered into the sitting room. 'Why, there you are, Professor. I've been looking for you all over the garden.'

'Could we have some coffee, please, Mrs Erskine?' he asked and then turned back to his visitor. 'Mr Fraddon, do sit down.'

'You're obviously making a splendid recovery,' said Fraddon heartily.

The professor made no immediate reply. Facing a life sentence of darkness and despair, he found the observation fatuous and insulting. And he resented such cheery bonhomie from a man who had just been snooping through his papers. He sat down in the arm chair beside the empty fireplace. 'I think I'm well enough to return to work.'

'Ah,' said Fraddon ominously. 'I wanted to talk to you about that.' He took a file on Professor Melmo from his briefcase. The professor was another of those lateral thinkers encouraged by the Minister to waste the public's money and annoy the Civil Service. At least this unruly boffin would no longer be a thorn in the bureaucrats' flesh. 'Now, I see you were seconded to the Atomic Energy Commission five years ago from Darlington University.'

The professor nodded.

'And you subsequently headed the research into automated control systems over at Duncaston. Until the accident.'

'I've been thinking about the accident,' interrupted the professor nervously. 'I believe I know what went wrong. I want to repeat the experiment.'

Mrs Erskine came into the room with coffee and biscuits which she placed on a table between the two men.

'Allow me,' said Fraddon. He pressed one cup into the professor's outstretched hand, and took another for himself. 'You know, this is absolutely idyllic.' He peered politely out at Fred Erskine's unkempt garden.

'How soon can I get back to the laboratory?' demanded the professor.

Fraddon looked grim. 'You were involved in a major accident.'

'I was not seriously irradiated.'

'You lost your sight, Professor! Now, the Department has, in the circumstances, agreed to a remarkably generous settlement.'

'I need to get back to my work!' pleaded the professor.

'Early retirement on a full pension.' Fraddon smiled. 'I must say, I envy you.'

The professor felt a tidal wave of depression flood over him. Since his wife, Marjorie's, death he had lived only for his work. Now, even that was in ruins. 'I take it,' he said stoically, 'that I am at least allowed to return to Darlington?'

'Any application will be given due consideration. But I must warn you that, in view of the sensitive nature of your recent work...'

This was worse than the professor had feared. It was the end of everything. 'Thank you so much for coming to see me,' he stammered. Raising himself from the chair, he staggered forward - straight into the coffee table. Table, tray, cups and professor crashed to the floor.

'Really, Professor!' fussed Mrs Erskine, running to see what all the noise was about.

Professor Melmo lay with his face to the carpet. 'Mr Fraddon is just going,' he explained quietly.

'Well, goodbye, Professor.' Fraddon closed his briefcase and walked with Mrs Erskine to the door.

'You all right?' said Mrs Erskine as she returned to the sitting room.

'Leave me alone,' said Professor Melmo miserably.

So Mrs Erskine, who knew better than to argue when the prof was in one of his moods, closed the door and went back to the kitchen.

Professor Melmo lay motionless in front of the fireplace while a purring Pythagoras lapped the spilt milk at his side. He tried to block out all consciousness, feeling, self awareness. To become part of an all-embracing black Universe. Slowly, the tension in his body ebbed away. As the pain of disappointment eased, he began to enjoy a most peculiar sensation of weightlessness. His body was like a helium balloon which proceeded to float, ever so gently, upward.

To his amazement and joy, the room into which he slowly rose was gradually filled with light. He blinked and stared at the familiar surroundings with new eyes. He noticed, with a tinge of embarrassment, the broken crockery and fallen table lying on the carpet. 'Hello there, Pythagoras.' He bent down to stroke the cat which had finished the milk and was licking its paws. But the professor's hand passed straight through the insubstantial animal. 'Am *I* a ghost, or are *you*?' he wondered. The question was swiftly answered by the sight of his *real* body, still lying beside the hearth.

The sitting room door would not open to his touch but he found himself able to pass quite smoothly through its wooden panels. He glided down the hallway, acutely aware of the ticking of the grandfather clock and the dappled sunlight which streamed from the window over the stairs. The door to the kitchen was open. Fred Esrkine had just come in from the back and was placing a plump, brown rabbit on the table. The creature's eyes were glazed, the fur behind its ears clogged with blood.

'That's kind, Fred,' said Mrs Erskine. 'Cheer the old boy up, a bit of rabbit. Just the job a rabbit pie.'

The professor turned away as Mrs Erskine picked up a large, sharp knife. He passed into the tiny study at the end of the passage.

Everything seemed in order: books, papers, his old Epson QX 10 shrouded in a plastic dust sheet. But all was not *quite* as he remembered it.

The blackboard on the wall beside the window had been filled with figures, letters and symbols – an enormous series of complex equations which he had never seen in his life before. His heart beat faster as he read through the proposition. What an amazing idea! For the first time since the accident at Duncaston he felt the creative adrenalin flow. Here was the basis of an entirely new line of experimentation.

He began to feel dizzy. The room spiralled . . .

'You all right in there, Professor?'

He was lying, stiff and cold, on the wet sitting room carpet. Unsighted, once more. He must have been hallucinating.

'Professor?'

He got to his feet and groped for the chair. 'Come in, Mrs Erskine.'

'Feeling better, then?'

'I think so.'

'Got a treat for your dinner. Fred's brought you a rabbit. Just the job, rabbit pie.' She righted the table and began to sweep up the shattered coffee cups.

The professor trembled with excitement. Perhaps he hadn't imagined it after all. He realised that he could still see, with an inner eye, the algebra from the blackboard. If only he could get it transcribed onto the computer. 'Mrs E!' He followed his housekeeper out into the hall. 'I need help with some calculations.'

'No good asking *me*, professor.'

'A student, perhaps?'

'What about Sylvia James's boy? Tolemy.'

'Does he understand advanced calculus?'

'He's blooming clever, I know that.'

'Very well. I must work with Tolemy James.' The professor seethed with impatience to transcribe the data from the board; data for the most amazing robotic design the world had known.

The little, baby heads popped, twelve at a time, from their extrusion pods. Bald as billiard balls, pink as Windolene, they tumbled to a waiting conveyor belt and thence to a cradle to be matched with their respective legs, torsos, arms and bundles of synthetic hair.

'These parts are for our Downee Dolls,' explained works manager, Bob Love, shouting to be heard over the gurgling of molten plastic and the gasp of compressed air. 'Cheap and cheerful, but quite popular with the less demanding sort of girl.' They moved on. 'Now we come to our Little Madam range with change of hair and clothes, and the usual incontinence facilities. Our best seller. A nice, traditional sort of doll.'

They turned into the next bay. 'This is our top line. The Swiss Miss. Full continental sophistication and a clockwork mechanism. The aristocrat of Tinkerbell Toys.'

Tolemy smiled at a tall, skinny boy, barely older than himself, who was sorting through a pile of high-heeled shoes. 'This is John Kirkwood,' said Bob. 'Our footwear specialist.' He chewed for a moment on his empty meerschaum and rattled the loose change in his baggy cords, then proceeded to introduce Tolemy to the denizens of other departments. There was Miss Tumber who did the little frocks and knickers, Mrs Reekie who delicately plumbed each miniature waterworks, Mr Liversage, the senior die-cast engineer, heading the small band of curious workers who welcomed Tolemy as their new employer.

'Let's go into the office,' said Bob. 'It's quieter in there.' The works manager gestured Tolemy towards a heavy swivel chair in front of a huge roll-top desk. 'You're the boss now, Tolemy.'

Tolemy sat down and surveyed his new headquarters. It was as eerily familiar to him as the rest of the factory. 'Who's that?' he pointed to a framed photograph on the wall. A rather fat man with long, grey hair was shaking hands with Princess Anne at the opening of Turlow Shopping Precinct.

'C.P., of course.'

'Who?'

'Old Charlie Protheroe, the gaffer – God rest his soul.' Bob looked puzzled. 'Isn't he a relative or something?'

'No,' said Tolemy plainly. 'I am here because I was chosen. For the work that must be done.'

'What work?' said Bob, removing the unlit pipe from his mouth.

'Excelsior!' cried Tolemy.

'I see,' said the works manager doubtfully, remembering the time C.P. got religion from Billy Graham at Wembley.

Hang on a moment, thought Tolemy to himself. *What the hell am I saying!*

Eddie, who wouldn't be seen dead with a doll, had got bored with the official tour and wandered off on her own. She now came into the office with Mrs Reekie and some tea. 'You're wrong,' she said, waving Tolemy's plan. 'About those alterations.'

'China cups,' whispered Mrs Reekie as she withdrew.

'I just got the time-scale wrong,' said Tolemy airily. 'The new workshop has not yet been built. But it soon will be.'

Bob Love's face was wreathed in smiles. 'Expansion? That's terrific. We were afraid you'd cut your losses and close us down. We'd have a snowball's chance getting new jobs in Turlow these days.'

Tolemy pointed to the architect's drawing. 'We'll need more assembly space here. New offices there . . .'

'Sounds to me as if you're going for a new model.'

'That's right. Something more technical. Computer chips and all that.' Tolemy outlined his scheme, trying hard to conceal the surprise he felt at his sudden intuition.

'Just a minute,' interrupted Eddie. 'What are you going to do for money?'

'Money will not be a problem,' Tolemy heard himself say.

'This new line,' said Bob Love. 'Will it be another doll?'

'A sort of a doll,' said Tolemy slowly. 'A walking, talking sort of a doll.' He smiled. Suddenly, he knew exactly what was to be done. 'We are going to build a robot!'

'I have a vision,' said General Spiby to the Minister as they sped down the motorway in the ministerial Rover.

'Oh, yes?' said the Right Honourable Justin Watkin, deep in the contents of his red dispatch box.

'Sir Bedevere, Sir Launcelot, Sir Galahad may yet return. The Knights of Arthur, in the armour of new technology, will save this troubled island.'

The Minister pretended he hadn't heard. Inwardly, he groaned. Spiby could be such an almighty bore. He should never have agreed to share his car.

'We may yet see a Britain that is truly Great,' said the general.

The minister noted, with relief, that they were already filtering left onto the Turlow spur. He also observed that his passenger had drawn a savage face in the margin of a confidential report.

'The new crusaders will be all-powerful, incorruptible.'

'You and your war machines!' The minister smiled.

'Machines that think. But know no fear, and cannot disobey.'

'These tests,' said the Minister. 'They won't go on all day, will they? My wife's got a dinner party, and she'll give me hell if I'm late.'

The car passed through the second security barrier at the end of a long unsurfaced road, bordered by a rough no-man's land of gorse and brambles. A guard checked their passes, saluted and waved them onto the main tank testing ground.

Turlow Heath was a barren tract of heather and scrub, hideously scarred by generations of mechanical monsters. In the centre of the area rose a solitary hillock, an oasis of grass and wild flowers, untouched by the depredations of military engineers.

Around the perimeter of the territory red warning flags waved in the breeze, declaring the zone out of bounds to all but the most senior personnel. Several vehicles were already drawn up in a rough corral alongside the guard room. A group of observers, some military, some civilian, stood drinking coffee beside the VIP refreshment wagon, talking in a babble of European languages. Technicians hovered in attendance, like altar boys, around a grey, unmarked van, the size of a small horse box which was parked a discreet distance from the rest of the staff cars.

'Good morning, Minister. Good morning, General.' Henry Fraddon, the senior civil servant from Special Projects, hurried across to greet the new arrivals. 'May I introduce Ms Charity O'Toole.' He gestured at an agressive-looking, ash-blonde female in a tight hounds-tooth skirt and blouse who was homing in on them like an Exocet. 'American liason.'

'Hi there, General. I'm sure looking forward to seeing your new baby.'

The general winced and turned away to a nervous, prematurely balding man who had just joined them. 'Hello, young Bidmead. Everything in order?'

'I hope so, sir.'

'Derek Bidmead, Head of Research,' muttered Henry Fraddon to the lady from the USA. 'Our leading computer expert.'

'Over to you, Derek,' said the general. 'And the best of luck.'

'Ladies and gentlemen. If you'd like to gather round . . .' The observers drifted towards the rear of the large, grey van. Derek Bidmead nodded to one of his acolytes at the rear of the pantechnicon. Slowly, the tailgate folded down to form a ramp from the floor of the vehicle to the ground, thereby revealing the contents of the interior.

At the top of the ramp stood something from an ironmonger's nightmare. It had a central body, square, like a water cistern and blistered with nodular appendages. Its head was a large goldfish bowl spiked with glass tubes like a supermarket security camera. It had four claw-like hands, two at the front and two at the rear. A pair of stumpy legs joined the main torso to the creature's broad, tank-track feet.

One of the civilians laughed.

'So this is your knight in shining armour?' said Justin Watkin to the general. 'The new Sir Galahad himself!'

'I am security android prototype zero one,' squawked a harsh, synthetic voice.

There was an appreciative murmur from the crowd.

'Why, isn't he cute?' said Charity O'Toole.

Derek Bidmead picked up a control box with a short aerial at the end. He pressed a switch. P Zero One jerked. The tank-tracks on his great, flat feet started to rotate. PZ1 staggered forward to the edge of the van, then, like a drunken old lady in carpet slippers, waddled down the ramp.

There was a round of applause. The Head of Research beamed like a proud father.

'Now what?' said the minister.

The android perambulated for about another hundred yards, then stopped. Its head spun round three times.

'Most impressive,' said Henry Fraddon sarcastically.

'Just you wait,' said General Spiby, leaning back on his shooting stick and admiring his protege through field glasses.

There was a roar from the direction of the guard house. Armed with sticks and stones and screaming like banshees, a platoon of soldiers invaded the testing ground.

'Here,' declaimed the general, 'we have your typical mob. Rioters, football hooligans, thugs from the SDP.'

'Stop, or you will be exterminated!' howled PZ1.

'What an original turn of phrase,' sniggered the minister.

The typical mob obligingly stopped.

'Mob, attack!' roared the general.

To the accompaniment of further bloodcurdling cries the rioters waved their sticks and threw their stones which clattered against the android's iron chest. One of the missiles hit a glass tube on the goldfish bowl and broke it off.

'I told you to avoid the scanning system!' protested the Head of Research.

'Exterminate! Exterminate!' screamed PZ1.

Derek Bidmead pressed another button on his control panel. Nozzles suddenly erupted like acne all over the automaton's skin. High powered jets of water coloured with red, blue and green dye spurted at the attackers who, as if on cue, fell to the ground. The onlookers quickly drifted sideways to avoid the technicolor drizzle which was now blowing in their direction.

'Second wave, attack!' ordered the general.

Another contingent advanced from behind the grassy knoll in the centre of the range. All the men carried guns.

'These are terrorists, rebels, dangerous pickets,' explained General Spiby. 'Insurgents, fire!' he commanded.

The soldiers let off a fusillade of blanks. An NCO threw a thunderflash. PZ1 wobbled about in the centre of the smoke, his four scarecrow arms waving like a couple of frantic tick-tack men. Bidmead pressed another switch.

Miniature cannon barrels bristled from the android's sides spraying plastic bullets over the heads of the attackers, all of whom had conveniently hit the deck.

The spectators clapped.

'Ever seen the finals of *Come Dancing*?' Fraddon asked his American colleague, with a sneer.

PZ1's globular head panned vigorously left and right as if at a tennis match. He confronted the ragged group of official spectators. 'Come forward with your hands up, or you will be exterminated!' The VIPs shuffled nervously, like reluctant children summoned on stage by a pantomime comedian. 'You have been warned!' shouted the android.

'Steady on, Bidmead,' growled the general. 'This isn't in the programme.'

The Head of Research was already busy with the switches of his mobile terminal. 'We're getting some sort of interference . . .'

'Ladies and gentlemen, I suggest we adjourn to the guard room,' the general warned.

Before anyone could move, there was another rattle of gunfire from the war machine. A hail of baton rounds now sprayed the distinguished observers. With screams of pain and terror the assembled company threw themselves into the heather.

'I warned you!' cried PZ1, trundling forward.

'Do something!' bellowed Spiby to the computer expert.

Bidmead pounded his keyboard like a demon organist, but to no avail. 'My signal's getting swamped,' he wailed. 'The machine is out of control!'

'Stop!' thundered the general, striding forward to the recalcitrant prototype and waving his shooting stick in the air.

'Silly old git!' screeched PZ1, dispatching a single plastic bullet.

Bellowing like a stuck rhinoceros, General Spiby rolled into the heather, hands to his groin.

'Good shot, PZ1,' said Henry Fraddon maliciously, from the safety of the refreshment truck.

'Exterminate! Exterminate!' Shells hurtled skyward from the android, bursting, like roman candles, into a myriad bright stars.

The hiding VIPs began to cough and wheeze. 'It's a gas attack!' yelled a German from NATO as the retching and choking spectators staggered from their cover.

'I am now armed with live ammunition,' announced the android.

'Don't panic!' cried a naval attache from Hilversum. But his voice was drowned by the screams of the Italians who had thrown caution to the winds and were running hell for leather to the guard house.

Sergeant Monk, who had been enjoying the discomfiture of the top brass enormously, now turned to his platoon. 'Right, you lot. We're going to sandbag Metal Mickey.'

'Get the hell out of here!' shouted Charity O'Toole to Henry Fraddon who was crawling on all fours beside the catering van.

'I've gone and lost one of my contact lenses,' he moaned.

There was another stacatto rattle from PZ1, combined with the whistle of real lead bullets.

The myopic Fraddon, now alone in the target area, screamed. An ugly stain slowly spread across the back of his pin-stripe jacket.

'Platoon, rapid fire!' ordered Sergeant Monk. From two flanks, the regular soldiers emptied their rifles at the android.

'Exterminate! Exterminate! Exterminate!' howled the machine, the pitch of its metal voice rising higher and higher. Smoke poured from its shattered modules. Green slime dribbled down its left leg. The cracked goldfish bowl wobbled on its broken neck. In a final gesture of defiance the prototype blasted a salvo of incendiary capsules at its attackers. The firebombs overshot their intended victims, falling instead around the minister's Rover. The limousine was instantly engulfed in flames. Moments later the petrol tank ignited with a shattering explosion.

There was a second detonation from the direction of PZ1 as Sergeant Monk lobbed a grenade at the stricken android. The would-be Sir Galahad was transformed into a heap of twisted, smouldering spare parts.

'You all right?' Charity O'Toole, her skirt torn, her eyes streaming, stumbled towards the prostrate Henry Fraddon.

'Get me an ambulance,' he whispered bravely. 'I've lost a lot of blood.'

'Just coffee,' explained the American, pulling her opposite number from under a punctured urn.

The civil servant got to his feet, trying to preserve what was left of his dignity and his suit. 'Thank you Ms. O'Toole.' He surveyed the carnage of Turlow Heath – and began to feel a great deal better. The experiment had been an even greater debacle than he dared hope. It would surely be curtains for those inconvenient inventors of the Annex.

'I take it,' he said to his companion, 'that you will be making a full report to Washington.'

'You bet your sweet life!' said Charity, unkindly.

Bidmead gazed, almost in tears, at the mangled corpse of PZ1.

'What the hell went wrong!' demanded the general, hobbling towards the Head of Research.

'Some sort of radiation,' stammered the distraught young man. He looked up at the grassy slope in front of them. 'I wonder...'

'That bloody hog's back? Been trying to get it levelled for years!'

Justin Watkin, hands in his pockets and a scowl on his face, strode from the wreckage of his car to that of the disastrous prototype. It had been the most traumatic morning of his life. 'Bit of a balls-up, eh Spiby?'

'Damned hill,' snorted the general. 'Deflected our control signals. Time we brought in the bulldozers.' There was a movement on the far boundary of the range. The general raised his binoculars. Something about the distant, blazered figure was unpleasantly familiar. 'It's the runt with the petition,' he expostulated. 'Hastie. That disgusting little man from the building society!'

Henry Fraddon strolled across to join the post mortem.

'What do *you* think, Henry?' said the minister, looking up from the most expensive heap of scrap in the county.

'I considered the project ill advised from its inception,' replied the civil servant, shaking his head.

'Spiby says we ought to get rid of that hill. Some sort of interference.'

'Out of the question, Minister. That *hill*, as you call it, is an Ancient Monument.'

'Indeed?'

'A long barrow. I believe the locals call it Tolemy's Tomb.'

Leslie Hastie put down his glasses. He had seen – and heard – enough to know that General Spiby's experiment had been a total disaster. Well, no one could say he hadn't warned them. He checked the latest ley line on his map. There was no doubt about it; the energy vector from the great hill at Silbury centred, like the other nine points of the Decagon, on the burial mound of Tolemy's Tomb. Looking back at the heath, Hastie could still see the general strutting about beside the barrow like a marionette, unaware of the primeval energy that flowed around him.

As he helped himself to a flask of tea and a Marmite sandwich from his haversack, Mr Hastie thought of the primitive builders of the tumulus; a race at one with the power of the Universe, and drawing that force to Earth. He thought of the genius of those Ancient Britons, born again in succeeding generations...

On the way home Tolemy began to have doubts. He'd sounded so sure of himself back at Tinkerbell Toys, but where on Earth would be find anyone with the technical know-how to build a full scale robot? And where would he find the money for such a massive project?

Terry James's lorry was already parked up in Beachcroft Close by the time Tolemy returned. The Erskines' vintage motorbike and side car were also standing outside the door of Number 3. Mr Erskine had obviously arrived for his weekly session on the pools with Mr James. Madge Erskine would be in the kitchen, gossiping with Tolemy's mum. He heard her voice as soon as he opened the front door.

'The tales I could tell you about the prof. Honestly, Sylve, you should have seen him this morning. Flat on the floor...'

'You back then, Tolemy?' Sylvia James was busy chipping potatoes as Tolemy came in from the hall.

'I'm starving,' said Tolemy, peering at a pound of sausages spitting under the grill.

'Listen to this, Tol,' said Madge. 'I've only gone and fixed you up with a job for the holidays.'

'I've already got a job at my factory,' said Tolemy grandly.

'I'll tell Professor Melmo you're too busy, then,' Madge Erskine winked at Tolemy's mum.

'Professor Melmo?' Tolemy vaguely remembered Mrs Erskine giving up her job alongside his mother at Woolies. Something to do with working for a man who'd gone blind. *Melmo*. Suddenly the name seemed both familiar and vitally important.

'At least go and see what he wants,' his mother suggested.

'He wants someone to help work his computer,' elaborated Mrs Erskine. 'I told him, "that Tolemy James is in his element with computers".'

'Okay,' said Tolemy and wandered through to the lounge to look for his father.

Terry James and Fred Erskine were poring over their football coupons. 'I reckon Manchester United and Charlton Athletic,' said Fred. 'Don't you?'

'Never,' said Terry. 'More like Sheffield Wednesday and Queens Park Rangers. What do you think, Tolemy?'

'Don't ask me.' Tolemy laughed. He knew as much about football as his father did about quantum physics.

'Go down to Droop Street, then?' Terry James asked casually.

'Yeah. Had a look.'

'Droop Street? What does the boy want in Droop Street?' demanded Fred, helping himself to another can of Tolemy's dad's 4X.

'I'm going to build a robot,' said Tolemy.

'Now there's a thing,' said Fred.

Terry James stared uneasily at his son. There were times when the boy seemed a complete stranger.

Tolemy's mum slid open the hatch. 'Will someone lay the table?' she shouted from the kitchenette.

'Clear the decks!' Tolemy broke up the pools syndicate to make way for the cloth.

'Here you are, Tol,' said Mrs Erskine, coming into the lounge with Professor Melmo's address on a piece of paper. 'Don't let me down, now.'

'Right, Madge. Get your crash helmet on,' ordered Mr Erskine, draining his beer.

As Fred Erskine's departing motorcycle combination clattered out of the Close, Tolemy stared at Mrs Erskine's scribbled directions. The professor lived out by the heath, only twenty minutes away. He made up his mind to go over in the morning.

As he placed the piece of paper on the middle shelf of the room-divider next to his father's completed football coupon, something drew his eyes to the printed lists of football teams. Something told him that the crosses his father had drawn were all in the wrong places. (Not that Tolemy could normally tell one end of a football coupon from the other.) In his mind's eye the boy saw the correct pattern of draws superimpose itself on the page.

He was on the point of sharing his remarkable insight when something made him hold his tongue. Such information was not for the likes of Mrs Erskine's Fred. Nor even his father. But what *was* the reason for such extraordinary precognition?

'What's all this about a robot?' said his dad.

'My robot? Of course!' In a flash, the reason for his valuable clairvoyance was made plain. This was how he would finance the work at Tinkerbell Toys.

'Remember,' said the Man in Black. 'All things are possible.'

He was surrounded by a company of armoured men, their plated bodies brilliant in the light of an eternal sun. *'Excelsior!'* they cried. 'We shall *become*!'

CHAPTER THREE

First thing next morning, Henry Fraddon from Special Projects was knocking on the door of the Right Honourable Justin Watkin.

'Well, Henry,' said the Minister, still smarting from the humiliation of the previous day (not to mention a sore backside from one of PZ1's plastic bullets). 'What's to be done?'

'Nothing precipitate, Minister,' said the civil servant, quietly planning the abolition of the Annex and the extermination of all its inhabitants. 'We must consider what is best for the Department.'

'Oh, quite. But what am I going to say to the Cabinet?'

'I suggest we announce a temporary suspension of tests, pending a detailed evaluation. For technical reasons.'

'Yes, yes, an inquiry. That's the thing.' The minister looked relieved.

'We may then have to reassess the feasibility of the whole programme.'

'Indeed we may,' agreed the minister enthusiastically. 'In the meantime, let's hope no one finds out how much that malevolent heap of ironmongery has cost the poor taxpayer.'

'Questions in the House?'

'Precisely.' Justin Watkin shifted uneasily, thinking of his slender majority. 'Damage limitation,' he concluded. 'Cut our losses. Perhaps you would explain the situation to General Spiby?'

Henry Fraddon smiled. 'It will be a pleasure, Minister.'

*

'There's nothing there!' Tolemy peered at the empty blackboard in the professor's study.

'There *must* be,' protested Professor Melmo obstinately. 'I saw it myself.'

'You *saw* it?' said Tolemy, staring sceptically at the blind scientist.

'In a manner of speaking.' The professor was reluctant to describe the extraordinary events of the previous morning.

But Tolemy was not to be put off. 'What do you mean *in a manner of speaking*?'

The professor was not used to being interrogated by fifteen-year-olds, but he needed to talk to *someone*. He began to explain what had happened to him on the sitting room floor.

'A classic case of astral projection,' said Tolemy, remembering his conversation with Eddie Fox. 'Your mind was separated from your body.'

'Impossible!' cried Professor Melmo, clinging instinctively to his scientific convictions. 'Mind and body are not divisible. Consciousness itself is a mere bi-product of neural activity.'

'Then how do you explain the rabbit that you *saw* in the kitchen?'

The professor shook his head. He had been trying to answer the same question. 'Very well,' he replied, grudgingly. 'Suppose we accept your hypothesis. Why is there now no writing on the board?'

'Someone came and wiped it off.'

'This room is kept locked and I have the only key.'

'Perhaps the information you thought you saw was only an intuitive projection,' replied Tolemy with a confidence that surprised even himself. 'Maybe some *entity* is trying to get in touch with you?'

'What makes you say that?'

'Because I believe *some entity* is trying to get in touch with *me*.'

Normally, the professor would have laughed at the boy. But, since yesterday, he was a wiser man. A light now shined in his inner darkness. He had, perhaps, discovered an entirely new way of *seeing*. Maybe he had even found a way out of his misery and a justification for his suffering.

'Can you still remember the formulae?'

'Perfectly.'

There was a click and a whirr; Tolemy had switched on the professor's micro-computer. 'Okay,' said the boy as the QX 10 booted up. 'Tell me exactly what is in your mind and I'll enter it into the machine.'

The professor began to reel off a complex string of letters and figures. Tolemy keyed in the opening equation, then paused to look at the screen.

'I'm sorry,' said Professor Melmo, hearing the rattle of the console stop. 'I'll go more slowly.'

'It's all right,' said Tolemy. 'I was just examining the proposition.'

'Don't waste time!' snapped the professor, impatient to get the information down onto disk. 'You can't possibly understand it anyway.'

'It's an analysis of non-linear robotic control,' answered Tolemy. 'A derivation of the Nyquist Array by the look of it.'

'What do you know about the Nyquist Array, young man?'

'I must have read something,' said the boy vaguely.

But the professor wasn't listening. He was transfixed by his vision of the formula on the blackboard. The characters had begun to spin like the information on an airport departure board. 'Quickly,' he shouted. 'Get this down!'

And so they continued, the boy typing to the older man's dictation. Line by line, the complex theorem diversified and expanded into a dimension which the scientist would never previously have comprehended.

After a couple of hours the professor slumped back exhausted. 'That'll do to be going on with.'

'What's wrong, Prof?' said Tolemy as they retired to the kitchen for a well-earned cup of coffee. 'You look depressed.'

'My dear boy. We've just evolved a design for the most advanced robotic experiment known to man. And there's no way I can use it.' The professor began to pour hot water from the kettle over the work surface. Tolemy gently guided his hand back to the cups. 'If only I were still working at Duncaston. Or even Darlington . . .'

'Come and work for me,' said Tolemy, kneeling to stroke the enormous ginger tom who was purring round his legs.

'I beg your pardon?'

'Tinkerbell Toys. I'm thinking of expanding into computer-controlled automata.'

'You!' exclaimed the professor. 'Build a robot? But...' The scientist was about to add that Tolemy was just a boy. But the older man had discovered, in the course of the morning, that his new friend was no ordinary teenager.

Tolemy took some milk from the fridge. 'What's your cat called, Professor?'

'Pythagoras,' murmured Professor Melmo, more confused than ever.

'Here you are, Pythagoras,' said Tolemy, pouring some milk into a saucer. He poured some more milk into their cups. 'I'd like you to start right away. 68, Droop Street.'

'But what about all the equipment? The organisation? The finance?'

'Leave that to me,' said Tolemy. 'Your job will be to design the robot. Do you want it or not?'

'My dear boy,' stammered Professor Melmo. 'I am entirely at your service.'

The perennial gloom of the Annex could do nothing to diminish Henry Fraddon's good humour as he hurried over with the bad news about the general's robot.

'PZ1 was sabotaged!' protested Spiby. 'That odious creature from the building society.'

'You may well be right, Arthur,' said Fraddon magnanimously. 'But that will be for the Inquiry to decide.'

As soon as he was alone, Spiby picked up the phone and dialled Scotland Yard. 'Inspector Cordingly, please. Special Branch.' While he waited for his former adjutant to answer the extension the general began to scribble angrily on a memo pad. Realising he had started to draw another brutal *face,* he stopped himself and turned his attention to the telephone. 'Good morning, Charles. Spiby,' he telegraphed in his inimitable style. 'Thirteen hundred hours. My club? Splendid. See you then.'

The general banged down the receiver, then tore the sheet from his jotter into tiny pieces. He peered out of the office window. Contrary to all evidence inside the Annex, it was a warm and sunny day. He decided he would leave early and walk to the rendezvous.

The old soldier strode briskly up Whitehall, thinking hard how best to outflank his political opponents. He scowled at a cluster of punks lounging beneath one of the lions of Trafalgar Square. What this country needed was more discipline! And fewer foreigners! He fought his way through a small army of Japanese tourists, across the road and into Pall Mall. Detective Inspector Charles Cordingly was already waiting in the hall when the general entered his club at a minute to one. 'Hello, Charles. Good of you to spare the time.'

'Not at all, sir,' said Cordingly who knew better than to disobey a summons from his old CO. 'What's the problem?'

The General described his vision of an army of robotic knights over whisky and soda in the club library. They then adjourned to the dining room where, across two bowls of peppery brown windsor, Inspector Cordingly was briefed on the unveiling of PZ1. An account of the android's disastrous disobedience on Turlow Heath accompanied a main course of overdone beef and waterlogged cabbage. Finally, as they demolished their bread and butter pudding and custard, the general voiced his fears for the future of Special Projects. 'Sorry to impose on you like this, Charles. But I need your help.'

Inspector Cordingly drained his glass of waspish claret and sipped his fudgy coffee. He could forgive Arthur Spiby just about anything, he decided, except this disgusting boarding school food. Next time the old boy needed a favour he could fork out on a decent restaurant. 'What exactly do you want me to do, General?'

'PZ1 was sabotaged. But I need to prove it.'

'Surely, it's for the technical boys to decide what went wrong.'

'Not *what*, Charles. *Who*!'

'Anyone in mind?'

General Spiby nodded. 'Some unspeakable conchie who lives in Turlow. I want him investigated. The name is Leslie Hastie.'

*

There was a man waiting on the doorstep of Number 3 when Tolemy got back to Beachcroft Close. He was quite old, with naff clothes and brylcreemed hair. A bit creepy, really - like a vicar without his dog collar. Perhaps he even *was* a vicar.

'Hello there!'

'What do you want?' said Tolemy, anxious to pick up some things and get over to Droop Street.

'My name is Hastie. Leslie Hastie. We're sort of neighbours.'

'Mum and dad are out at work.'

'It's you I want to see, *Tolemy.*'

Tolemy shivered. The man - this perfectly unassuming wally - had spoken his Christian name as if it were a curse.

'Don't look so surprised. I heard you talking to your friend, down by the canal.'

'You were fishing,' remembered Tolemy.

'Fishing for clues. My research.'

'What research?' asked the boy, wondering if his visitor were some kind of scientist.

'I need to know,' said Mr Hastie enigmatically, 'why your father christened you Tolemy.'

Tolemy took Mr Hastie into the kitchenette and put on the kettle. He decided it wouldn't matter if he were a few minutes late meeting the professor at Tinkerbell Toys. '*Tolemy* just came into my dad's head. So he says, any road.'

'Perhaps he was thinking of Tolemy's Tomb?'

Tolemy felt an electric charge shoot down his spine. 'What's Tolemy's Tomb?'

'A burial mound in the centre of Turlow Heath. We believe it to be a reservoir of cosmic energy.'

'Don't think my dad knows much about cosmic energy.' Tolemy slowly spooned some Maxwell House into a couple of mugs, wondering if he'd brought a nut case into the house. 'Who's *we*?'

'Beg pardon?'

'You just said "we believe".'

'We are Ley Hunters. We follow the highways of primitive man.'

'Oh?' Tolemy was none the wiser.

'It's quite simple.' Mr Hastie took an ordnance survey map from his blazer pocket and spread it on the formica top. 'First you identify the sites of ancient sanctity.' He ringed the locations of a couple of Saxon churches, a Roman temple and half a dozen more archaeological features on the large scale chart. 'Can you see a pattern, Tolemy?'

'Of course.' Tolemy traced a straight line, with his finger, between five of the sites.

'That's what we call a ley line.' Mr Hastie joined up the circles with his propelling pencil.

'Looks just like a road to me,' said Tolemy with a quick glance at the kitchen clock.

'Leys are more than roads,' said Mr Hastie. 'They are lines of elemental power, through which primitive man was in touch with the forces of the Earth, the spirit of the Universe.'

'And Tolemy's Tomb?'

'The tomb is at the centre of a vast force field. But I need a larger map to explain. Come round to my bungalow sometime.'

Tolemy would normally have dismissed Mr Hastie as a harmless loony. But something about his account of ancient powers intrigued the boy.

'The end of Ossington Lane. Any day will do.'

'You on the dole, then?' said Tolemy. 'That's tough.'

'Retired,' Mr Hastie quickly corrected him. 'Thirty-six years with the TBS.'

'The building society?' Suddenly Tolemy, who had been wondering how to convert his advance knowledge of the football results into cash, had a brilliant idea. 'Can you do me a favour?' He pulled a piece of paper from the back pocket of his jeans. 'I need someone over eighteen to handle some finance. And you being a businessman . . .'

'Investing your pocket money? Most prudential,' said Leslie Hastie approvingly.

Tolemy placed the paper together with a few coins in Mr Hastie's hand. 'I've worked it out on my computer. Should make about a million quid.'

Mr Hastie stared at the completed football coupon.

'Ask them to make the cheque out to Tinkerbell Toys.'

Mr Hastie gulped.

'Talking of which' – Tolemy looked guiltily back at the clock – 'I'm late for an appointment with my new Director of Research.'

Tolemy walked with Leslie Hastie down to the front gate and into the close. 'Do you really think there's a connection between me being called Tolemy and this burial thing on Turlow Heath?'

'I believe in the possibility of folk memory,' said Mr Hastie. 'A primeval unifying force acting across time.' He watched the extraordinary young man cycle off towards the main road. Then he carefully folded Tolemy's football coupon, placed it in his wallet, and set off for the nearest post office.

Tolemy arrived at Tinkerbell Toys to find the whole factory buzzing with anticipation. The assembly line had stopped. 'Orders of the governor,' declared Mr Liversage to a bemused workforce as he stripped out the old moulds. 'We're tooling up for a new model.'

Professor Melmo had already installed himself in the cluttered manager's office where Bob Love was busy cabling up the prof's QX 10 which had accompanied its owner to the factory in a minicab. The taxi driver staggered in with a graphics printer. 'Where do you want this lot, mate?' Bob Love cleared a pile of old ledgers from the top of a filing cabinet.

'Coffee! Strong! Black!' barked the professor, brushing aside Mrs Reekie's offer of a cup of tepid Typhoo.

'Hello, Professor,' said Tolemy to his Head of Research.

'What kept you?' said Melmo crustily.

'Sorry,' said Tolemy. 'I had some business with our Finance Controller.'

'In which case,' replied the professor, 'you are entirely excused.' He felt for the switch on the side of his QX 10 and the computer bumbled into life. 'Money is a commodity we shall require by the bucket-full.'

Bob Love chewed the stem of his cold meerschaum, juggled a handful of coins in his pocket and ruminated. (Bob was a compulsive ruminator). How could a child pay for all these new developments? Tinkerbell Toys, as the

Works Manager well knew, was virtually bankrupt.

The first of many intricate plans soon came rolling out of the professor's laser printer. It was the design for a section of the robot's wrist and forearm. Bob Love stared in awe at the complex blueprint. 'This is no ordinary toy,' he muttered.

'Of course it's not a toy!' snapped Melmo.

'It's a robot,' said Tolemy.

Bob Love suddenly began to feel as excited as if he had just discovered a rare loco for his old Hornby train set. All the knowledge and skill he had acquired from years of night school, countless extension courses at the tech, his Open University BSc could now be put to proper use. Equally swiftly (Bob was a compulsive pessimist), his natural caution reasserted itself. 'This fellow will need a lot of special components.'

'Give me a list of what you require.'

'Not to mention a backpack of megabyte chips.'

'All things are possible,' said Tolemy.

'I hope you're right,' said Bob Love dourly. He tapped the empty bowl of his pipe on the side of a filing cabinet and hurried away to check where the wall would be knocked down to make way for the extension.

Tolemy keyed some more instructions into the professor's PC and started to print another drawing. There followed another, and then another. Precise specifications for a thousand grippers and graspers, fingers and photosensors, tendons and torque exchangers, conduits and actuators, capacitive perceivers and prosthetic skin. By the time evening came, both Tolemy and the professor were exhausted. 'Let's get some fresh air,' said Professor Melmo.

They walked along the bank of the canal, the blind man's right hand resting lightly on the boy's arm. 'Remember,' said the scientist. 'To every action there is an equal and opposite reaction.'

'What do you mean?'

'The world is a terrible place.' He stood still for a moment, listening to the water sluicing through the lock gates and thinking of his wife Marjorie, slaughtered on a fog-bound motorway. 'Power and knowledge can be used in so many ways. For good or for ill.'

'Excelsior,' said Tolemy, quietly.

The professor laughed. 'You really are the most ridiculously optimistic young man I ever met.' They had arrived at the back garden of a small canalside pub. 'Unfortunately, my dear boy, much as I would enjoy some refreshment, you are too young to go to the bar and I am only too likely to spill our drinks.'

The problem was swiftly solved. 'Hi, Tolemy!' Roy Smart, a technician from Tinkerbell Toys, had already spotted the new arrivals. 'Want some help?' The young man obligingly took their orders and went into the Fisherman's Arms.

The blind man sat quietly in the setting sun, marvelling at the great algebraeic constellation that now shone in the inner space of his mind. 'There is a *force,*' said the scientist. 'Where does it come from?'

'Not from this world,' said Tolemy, gazing up at the infinite blue sky.

Roy Smart came back into the garden with a tray of glasses. 'Cheers,' said Tolemy, taking a Coke for himself and a pint of bitter for the prof.

'Good luck, Tolemy,' said Roy, giving the professor some change and returning to his companion on the other side of the lawn.

'Thanks, Roy.' Sergeant Jimmy Monk sipped the lager his brother-in-law had just brought back from the bar. He stretched himself as best he could in the rickety pub chair, glad to be out of uniform with a spot of leave ahead. 'That's never your new boss?' He gestured to the teenager in earnest conversation with the older man beyond them.

'That's Tolemy,' said Roy Smart.

'Bit wet behind the ears.'

'The kid's got a few ideas, I tell you, Jimmy. We're only going to build some sort of robot.'

'I could tell you a few things about robots,' said the sergeant. And he did, sending his brother-in-law into fits of laughter as he described the antics of PZ1 on Turlow Heath. 'They said it was some kind of interference from the burial mound.'

'Hidden metal?' suggested his brother-in-law.

'You should have seen the Top Brass scarper when they

started getting flack up the bum!'

'You get a lot of metal in old burial mounds,' said Roy Smart. 'I've read about it in the papers. People have found gold and silver and jewellery worth millions of pounds.'

'Is that a fact?' said the sergeant thoughtfully.

'People will laugh at you now,' said the Man in Black. 'But soon you will have power over Princes and Presidents.'

Tolemy saw, in his dream, that behind his ghostly mentor there stood an army of silver warriors.

'Use that power well, Tolemy,' said the Man in Black.

'Where have you been all weekend!'

'Working,' said Tolemy, collapsing into a chair in the Foxes' kitchen.

'It's supposed to be the holidays,' said Eddie Fox indignantly.

'I've been at the factory.'

'Doing what?'

'Really, Edwina, don't be so inquisitive,' said Mrs Fox, busy slicing aubergines for a *ratatouille*.

'I told you. I'm building a robot.'

'Where do you get all these mad ideas?'

'I don't know really,' whispered Tolemy, anxious to talk – though not to Mrs Fox. 'Those dreams. I don't know whether it's some sort of hallucination or...'

'There's this old woman who keeps coming into Citizens' Advice,' said Eddie spitefully. 'Thinks she's Margaret Thatcher.'

'Perhaps she *is*.'

'She's schizophrenic,' interrupted Mrs Fox. 'And that's no laughing matter.'

'*I'm* not schizophrenic,' said Tolemy defiantly. He lay back and closed his eyes. It had been an exhausting three days. Closeted with Professor Melmo in the poky Droop Street office, he had printed page after page of intricate designs and circuits from the alien data in the computer. The final blueprint was virtually complete. He needed only to assemble the necessary components and construction of the most sophisticated man-machine ever conceived could begin. Not that that was going to be easy.

'Is your dad in?'

'So that's why you came round,' said Eddie resentfully. 'Might have known you had an ulterior motive.'

The last thing Tolemy wanted was a row with his best friend. 'Come round to the factory,' he suggested generously.

'Spend the holidays in that grotty dump? You've got to be joking!'

'What time's supper? I'm famished.' The tall, bearded figure of Mr Fox came in from the garden. 'Hello, Tolemy!' Bernard Fox was always delighted to see his star pupil.

'Tolemy's building a robot,' said Mrs Fox, tossing vegetables in her new wok over the hob.

'That's a splendid holiday project,' said Mr Fox, wishing that Edwina would show half as much initiative.

'I was wondering, sir – I mean, Mr Fox . . .' Tolemy had to remind himself that they were not in the classroom.

'*Bernard*, please,' said Mr Fox, adding to the boy's confusion.

'I was wondering if I could use the school computer again. There's a rather complicated programme I want to run.'

'Course you can, old chap. Get the key from the caretaker's office. Tell old Scragg you've got my permission.'

Tolemy was relieved that Mr Fox had not asked him too many questions. He would rather not explain that he needed the school's telephone modem for some important long-distance hacking.

'Are you staying for supper, Tolemy?'

Tolemy suddenly realised he hadn't eaten all day. 'Thanks, Mrs Fox.'

'Of course,' said Mr Fox authoritatively, when they were all seated round the kitchen table, 'the idea of a robot as a cognitive, surrogate human is pure science fiction.'

'Do you think so, Mr Fox – Bernard?'

'Absolutely.' The science teacher poured Tolemy a small glass of Spanish Rioja. 'The technology – the designs for co-ordination and recognition are just not available.'

Tolemy thought of Professor Melmo, still at work in the old factory by the canal.

'We won't get your *Doctor Who* robot in my generation.

Though I dare say you and Eddie will live to see the day.' Mr Fox smiled patronisingly. 'Of course, if there's anything I can do to help...'

'Know anything about ley lines?' said Tolemy, swiftly changing the subject.

'Load of bunk,' declared Mr Fox unequivocally. 'Pseudo-scientific gobbledegook.'

'Isn't there some times an *element* of truth in pseudo-science?'

Bernard Fox laughed. 'The idea that primitive man erected great piles of stones all over the British Isles and used them to communicate with creatures from Outer Space is perfectly ludicrous.' He poured himself some more wine. 'You take my advice, old chap. Stick to building your Meccano man!'

Roy Smart had been shopping at the Tandy store in the Precinct. He said nothing about the purchase to his wife Eileen and hid the wrapped, oblong package in the cupboard under the stairs. After tea on Sunday, as soon as Mrs Smart had left to visit her mother over in the Old Town, Roy retrieved the parcel from behind a pile of suitcases and a broken-down hoover and brought it into the living room. Jimmy Monk, who was spending the weekend with his brother-in-law, helped him open the box and remove the blocks of polystyrene wadding. Roy lifted out a black, circular disc into which he inserted a long plastic handle.

'Just like a mine detector,' observed Sergeant Monk.

'Same thing, really. Makes a noise when you hold it above anything metallic.' Roy consulted the accompanying instructions and pressed a switch on the underside of the handle. As he slowly passed the device over the armchair beside the fire, the machine whistled. Roy slipped his hand down the side of the chair and pulled out a two pence piece. 'What did I tell you?'

Jimmy Monk agreed that the equipment was exactly what they needed for their forthcoming expedition.

'A simple metal detector,' said Roy, putting the device back in its box ready to go in the boot of the car. 'No treasure hunter should be without one!'

*

'Thanks for supper, Mrs Fox.'

Tolemy would have liked to have stayed longer at *Westaways*, but Mr Hastie had telephoned earlier in a state of some excitement and the boy had promised to call in on his eccentric new friend in Ossington Lane. Eddie, who told her father they were off to play ping-pong at St Swithin's Church Hall, insisted on coming with him.

'Come in! Come in!' Leslie Hastie greeted his visitors in a flapping cardigan at the door of his bungalow. 'Heard the results, young Tolemy?'

'No.'

'Your Triple Chance. I checked it on the wireless. Correct to the last detail. Quite amazing.'

'Oh, that.' Tolemy was unsurprised at the news.

'What's he talking about?' whispered Eddie. Football pools were an entirely unknown quantity at *Westaways*.

'Company finance,' Tolemy replied dismissively as they went inside.

Mr Hastie's heavy dining room table was crowded with maps and guide books and geometric instruments. Back numbers of *Ley Hunters' World*, *Vegetarian Monthly* and *Psychic News* were stacked around the floor like tottering skyscrapers. Leslie Hastie spread the *Readers' Digest* Map of Historic England and Wales open on the table. 'Now,' said Leslie Hastie. 'Just have a look at this.'

Tolemy and Eddie squinted at the network of superimposed lines and intersections that had been plotted and drawn by the devoted ley hunter. The locations of ten ancient monuments in various corners of the kingdom had been highlighted in yellow day-glow ink. Connecting lines joined each together forming a regular, ten-sided figure. 'You see,' said Mr Hastie. 'A perfect Decagon.' Radials had been drawn from each of the ten points, inwards to the centre, the ten spokes aligning other historical sites (which had been highlighted in red). The blue circle at the centre point was just to the east of Turlow New Town. 'There it is, at the heart of the whole system,' said Mr Hastie as if he were revealing the Holy Grail. 'Tolemy's Tomb. A reservoir of enormous – I suspect even dangerous – orgone energy.'

'He's off his trolley!' whispered Eddie as Leslie Hastie

went to fetch another book for Tolemy's inspection. 'Let's get away from here.'

But Tolemy would not move. He *could* not move. His eyes were riveted on the geometric figure on the map. There were goose pimples on his arm, his scalp tingled. The pattern of lines spiralled. He felt that if he stepped forward he would disappear into the centre of the Decagon.

'Come on, Tolemy!' Eddie had just thought of a plan to escape both from Mr Hastie and the lecture on his silly hobby.

'What?' Tolemy pulled himself together.

'Let's go and have a look at your famous tomb.'

'But Turlow Heath belongs to the army. It's a prohibited area.'

'That's what you think,' said Edwina Fox.

It was getting dark as Roy Smart drove with his brother-in-law along the narrow lane which bordered Turlow Heath. They passed a track leading to the main guardhouse, the barrier locked and surrounded with grim warnings from the Ministry of Defence. About half a mile further on, Jimmy Monk slowed down and peered ahead into the gloom. 'Coming up now, on the left.'

Roy slowed the car and pulled into a rough layby, overhung with trees. A family of rabbits froze, caught in the headlights, scampering off as the two men climbed from the vehicle. Roy opened the boot and handed his brother-in-law two long bundles wrapped in black bin-liners. Gathering up a couple of rubber-handled torches, he gave one to Jimmy and slammed the boot shut.

The two men pushed their way through the undergrowth in the direction of the perimeter fence. Roy felt distinctly nervous – as if the thick strands of barbed wire that appeared before them as they broke through a clump of hazel trees were the Berlin Wall itself. He expected, at any moment, searchlights and the rattle of machine guns.

'Don't look so worried,' said the sergeant. 'It's a weekend. The whole place is deserted.' He took a pair of wire cutters from the pocket of his combat jacket and smartly severed three strands of wire. He coiled the slack to one side and led the way through the gap onto the testing ground.

Tolemy's tomb rose like a great galleon about a hundred yards in front of them, backlit by the luminous evening sky. They walked steadily towards the mound, over the flat, track-scarred earth. It was a barren, deserted place. The distant traffic, the faint barking of a dog, sounded a million miles away.

At the bottom of the hill the two men stopped and put down their bundles. Roy took his metal detector from one of the plastic bags. From the other the sergeant extracted a couple of spades. 'Okay. Let's work our way round the outside, then up to the top.'

Roy Smart was suddenly filled with dread. The great, black mass beside him seemed to become a living thing – a huge, black killer whale that might, at any moment, turn and devour them. But the young man said nothing, for fear of being laughed at by the soldier. The wave of panic receded and he switched on the machine.

Leaving their tools on the ground the two men began a slow tour of the base of the mound with the metal detector held in Roy's hand, a few inches above the grass. All was silent except for the faraway rattle of a train.

'Are you sure this thing's working?'

Roy raised the detector to Jimmy's wrist. There was a bleep as it sensed the metal of his watch.

'Okay, okay.'

They set off on another silent circuit, higher up the grassy knoll with Jimmy Monk in charge of the detector. Some half an hour later, hot and breathless, they had reached a point three quarters of the way up the hill without so much as a squeak from the machine. They began to wish they had stayed at home and watched the movie on TV.

They were within six feet of the summit when the detector began to whistle like a kettle coming to the boil. Jimmy panned the device to one side – and the oscillation surged. 'Go and get the spades!'

Tolemy and Eddie hid their bicycles under some bushes just off the road, then scrambled through a dark tunnel of shoulder-high bracken towards the tank testing ground. Eddie confidently led the way to a section of the fence where the lower strand of barbed wire sagged like a skipping rope.

'How did you know about this?' said Tolemy, easing himself through the gap.

'A lot of girls from the sixth form come up here.' Eddie wriggled her way through into the forbidden zone.

'Why?'

'Don't be so dumb, Tolemy!' She laughed.

The near darkness had turned the ravaged heath into an alien landscape on which the ghostly criss-cross of tank trails stood out like the canals of Mars. Tolemy shivered.

'There's your tomb.'

In front of them loomed a great, black shadow. It was the prehistoric burial chamber, erected three thousand years before by a long-dead race. Tolemy walked blindly forward, lured by the massive nexus of energy. An owl swooped, screeching, across the heath.

'I think we ought to go back!' Eddie was frightened.

But there was no going back. The time had come for Tolemy to meet his destiny.

'Tolemy!' Eddie grabbed the boy by the arm. 'There's someone up there!'

Roy and Jimmy, frenziedly digging, had no inkling of the watchers in the darkness below. The sergeant held the metal detector over the hole which had been driven four, sweated, back-breaking feet into the soil. The device screamed. 'We're nearly there, old son!' He drove his spade once more into the earth. There was a dull crack as it impacted with a solid object. 'Bingo!'

Roy leaped excitedly into the shallow excavation. He, too, felt the hard, even surface a few inches below his spade. For several miutes more both men shovelled frantically. 'Let the dog see the rabbit.' Jimmy Monk shone a torch into the hole. Something reflected flat and grey beneath their feet.

Another ten minutes and the outer edges of the object had been cleared. The treasure hunters dug carefully around the four sides to reveal what looked like an oblong box. 'She's coming!' Jimmy pushed the object from side to side like a loose tooth. More earth was removed.

'Steady, now. Don't want to damage anything.' The two men leaned down and, each grasping two corners, hauled at the box. Slowly the remaining soil released its hold. Roy and Jimmy staggered to the side of the hole and placed their prize on the grass. Roy cleaned the surface dirt with his spade while Jimmy held the torch.

They gazed at a stone casket the size of a small hifi loudspeaker. There was writing on the surface, but not in any language known to Jimmy or Roy.

Ειμι προ Ητολεμη
μουον Ητολεμη
δρα πας ζνος

'Hope it's not a load of old bones,' said Jimmy Monk anxiously.

His brother-in-law picked up the detector and held it against the sides of the box. There was a reassuring howl from the machine. 'That's metal, all right!'

There was no obvious sign of a lid. 'Stand back!' Jimmy raised his spade over his head.

'Steady on, Jim.' Something made Roy Smart uneasy. He felt – though only vaguely – that their treasure trove deserved a measure of respect.

Not so the sergeant. 'No point in messing about!'

The flash that followed turn night into day, like the prime moment of an atomic explosion. Eddie and Tolemy turned away from the cold, blinding light and dropped, terrified, into one of the deep ruts. They held their hands over their ears to blot out the high-pitched wail that accompanied the lurid phosphoresence and the screams of the two unfortunate humans who had violated the tomb.

As the luminence grew less intense, Tolemy dared to look back at the mound. The two treasure hunters stood, rigid as scarecrows, on the peak. Such was the unnatural radiation that the bones of the men shone right through their clothes and flesh. Gradually, the light dimmed and the two tormented skeletons fell to the ground. Tolemy got to his feet. He knew that the danger was over.

Leaving a still terrified Edwina cowering on the heath, the boy climbed the slope. He observed – quite dispassionately – that two piles of empty clothes were all that remained of the diggers on the hill. He looked at the object which had been revealed. Then, certain beyond all doubt what was required of him, Tolemy James picked up the sarcophagus.

'It was horrible,' said Tolemy to the Man in Black.

'The desire for power and wealth can, indeed, be a terrible thing. But you must learn and profit from the experience.'

'Profit? You mean the casket?'

'Take good care of that box, Tolemy James,' said the Man in Black.

CHAPTER FOUR

The young man from the Pools Company arrived outside Mr Hastie's bungalow first thing on Monday morning in a chocolate Ford Granada. 'A cheque for one million, two hundred thousand pounds and forty three pence will be handed over at a star-studded presentation,' announced the executive.

'No publicity, if it's all the same to you,' replied Leslie Hastie.

'They all say that.' The man from the pools flashed his pearly teeth. 'But our winners can't usually resist a celebration with the likes of Michael Aspel or Terry Wogan.'

'No publicity,' repeated Mr Hastie obstinately. 'It says so on the form.'

'Bruce Forsyth?' The man from the pools made his final offer.

'Definitely no publicity,' insisted Mr Hastie. 'You can make the cheque out now to the Turlow Building Society. For the account of Tinkerbell Toys.'

Leslie Hastie finished his breakfast, then caught the bus into town. He dropped a hold-all of dirty washing into the Dolly Tub and sauntered over to the offices of the Turlow Building Society. 'Morning, Miss Powell. Morning, Mrs Smart,' he greeted his former colleagues behind the counter. (Mrs Smart, he noticed, looked rather under the weather.)

'How you doing, Leslie?' The pushy new manager, Kevin Kettle, waved from his inner sanctum.

Mr Hastie handed over the largest deposit Miss Powell

had ever seen and set off for Droop Street to tell Tolemy his money was in the bank.

Tolemy let himself in to the school's computer room with the key he had borrowed from Mr Scragg the caretaker. He wondered, for a moment whether to lock the door behind him, but decided it would only invite suspicion. In any event, it was unlikely that the headmaster - whose caravanette he had spied in the car park - would come visiting the shrine of New Technology. (The headmaster was a closet computer hater.)

Tolemy switched on a BBC Acorn and plugged the modem into the RS232 port at the rear. The micro was now hard-wired to British Telecom, and the world was at his fingertips - as was over a million, computer-accessible pounds at the Turlow Building Society.

It was quite fun being stinking rich. But Tolemy knew that the money had been given for a purpose - as had the stone casket from the tomb, now safely hidden under the compost behind Terry James's garden shed. He reached for his new, pink, plastic briefcase and extracted a wadge of computer paper. This was his first shopping list - some of the new components and materials needed by Professor Melmo and Bob Love back at Droop Street. It was a very long list indeed.

He put the computer on line and accessed a firm in California, USA. He tapped out his requirements, gave delivery information and invoice details, and the deal was done. Tolemy felt quite absurdly pleased with himself. He entered another code into the Acorn - and was through to Japan where he requisitioned about a hundred thousand pounds worth of the latest integrated circuits as casually as if they were plug-in ROM cards from the hobby shop in the precinct. Next stop Hamburg, and an order for a rare alloy. Then to Milan for optical fibres, Toulouse for servo motor units, Birmingham for plastic compound.

By the end of the morning he had travelled, electronically, several times round the globe - and had made a large dent in his account at the building society. (Though there was sure to be more where that came from.)

The door of the computer room opened. 'Tolemy!'

'Oh, hello, sir.' It was Mr Attwood, the headmaster. Tolemy shuffled his notes out of sight.

'Doing some holiday work?'

Tolemy sent up a silent prayer that Mr Attwood wouldn't ask any awkward questions. 'Just trying out a program. Bernard – Mr Fox said it would be all right.'

'Jolly good. Jolly good.'

Tolemy observed, with relief, that Mr Attwood was wearing the crimplene safari suit he reserved for Saturdays and holidays and was thus unlikely to have arrived on official business.

'We've got high hopes for you, young Tolemy.' Mr Attwood edged towards the computer as if obliged to show an interest. 'University, even.'

Tolemy took evasive action. 'You know all about Latin and Greek, don't you sir?' He took from his case a piece of paper on which he had copied the inscription from the sarcophagus.

ειμι προ ητολεμη
μουον ητολεμη
δρα πας ζνος

'Can you tell me what this means?'

The headmaster, who was only too glad to avoid revealing his ignorance about computing matters, happily perused the paper. 'Eimi pro Ptolemy monon Ptolemy hora pas allos.' He pondered for a moment. 'How curiously runic.'

'Sir?'

'I am for Ptolemy, and Ptolemy alone. Beware all others,' Mr Attwood translated. 'Where did you find this?'

'Oh, on a tomb,' said Tolemy candidly.

But Mr Attwood had graver matters on his mind. He looked anxiously round the room, then went and unlocked a metal cupboard from which he extracted a video camera and portable VHS.

Tolemy, who was still on line to Sydney, with a few more keystrokes, confirmed another order. He tried to block Mr

Attwood's view of the screen – and the information that ten thousand Australian dollars had just been spent on an advanced image processing unit.

He needn't have bothered, for the headmaster had no interest in the details on the VDU. 'Must dash. Rehearsal for *The Sound of Music*.' (Mr Attwood was a leading light with the Turlow Amateur Operatic Society.) 'Keep it up, Tolemy,' he let himself out with a wave and a smile at the door. 'Jolly good!'

Tolemy breathed a sigh of relief. He took the piece of paper, and, while the words were fresh in his mind, wrote in the headmaster's translation. *I am for Ptolemy and Ptolemy alone*. The message from across the centuries confirmed what he had known instinctively on the heath. That he was *meant* to possess the casket from the burial mound. It was all part of the plan.

Tolemy folded the paper and put it back in his pink case. He turned, once more, to the computer and accessed San Diego.

That same morning, Kevin Kettle, the bright, new manager of the Turlow Building Society had a most unexpected visitor.

'Inspector Cordingly, Special Branch. Just a routine inquiry.'

But Kevin Kettle was a man of the world and a Rotarian and knew perfectly well that officers from Special Branch did not get sent on routine inquiries. Kevin Kettle had also been speaking to Superintendant Wally Bellis at Turlow police station (on behalf of poor Mrs Smart) and had heard a whisper of funny business on the testing ground. 'I suppose it's about yesterday's carry-on up at the Heath?' said Kettle, giving the inspector his penetrating look.

'What makes you think that?'

'Turlow's a small town. Word soon gets round the professional classes. I play golf with the local Super,' he added with a subtle wink.

'Tell me what you know,' said Cordingly, hiding his own ignorance.

'Just that a couple of blokes did a bunk. Left all their clothes on the tank testing ground. Money, shoes, Y-fronts, the lot. I take an interest, Inspector, because Roy Smart's wife is one of my cashiers.'

Inspector Cordingly quietly filed the information away in his mind, to check later with the MoD. 'Actually, I wanted to have a word with you about Leslie Hastie.'

'Leslie?'

'I gather he used to work here?'

'Well, yes.'

'Why did Mr Hastie retire so early?'

'Leslie had a lot of outside interests. Besides, he wasn't very happy with the new set-up here. Since we went over to computers.' Kevin Kettle leaned back in his chair and pitched into a dazzling dissertation on the merits of electronic banking systems.

'When did you last see him?' Cordingly interrupted.

'This morning, as it happens.' Kettle struggled to remember an earlier conversation with Gwyneth Powell. 'Depositing some money.'

'Indeed?'

The manager keyed the terminal on his desk - and gasped at the figures which flickered onto the screen. 'Over a million quid!'

That afternoon, Tolemy addressed the entire workforce of Tinkerbell Toys. To an accompaniment of much crashing and banging from the workmen extending the main assembly shed, he explained about the new man-machine. He promised lavish bonuses provided they all worked hard and kept their mouths shut. There was a round of applause as the boy finished speaking.

After the meeting, Tolemy put through a quick call to *Westaways* where a rather frosty Mrs Fox explained that Eddie didn't want to speak to him. 'I don't know what's been going on, Tolemy, but the poor girl's terribly upset.'

Tolemy blushed scarlet and, mumbling a few half-baked excuses, put down the phone. Mrs Fox had got the wrong end of the stick. But he could hardly explain what really happened on Turlow Heath.

He wandered out into the yard to examine the new portacabin that had been delivered and set up that morning. A young woman had already made herself at home inside and was examining a sheaf of plans for the new robot. She wore green high-heeled shoes and a dress like a large black dishcloth. Her hair was bright red. 'Who are you?' said the Toyah Willcox lookalike.

'Tolemy James.'

'Hi. I'm Hodge.'

'Just Hodge?' said Tolemy.

'Just Hodge. Like Madonna,' said Hodge.

'This apparition, by the way, is Hodge,' explained Professor Melmo, tapping his way into the cabin. 'Hodge is a computer genius from Darlington.'

'What do you think?' said Tolemy, pointing to the plans of the robot's micro-circuitry.

'Where did you nick them from?'

Tolemy was appalled. 'We worked them out ourselves. Me and the prof.'

'Bugger me!' said Hodge. 'You've only gone and got hold of the format for a sixth - maybe even *seventh* generation computer. That research is at least ten years ahead of anything I've heard of. And *I* haven't just arrived on a banana boat!'

The professor smiled quietly to himself. It was going to be fun working with Hodge again.

She looked again at the plans. 'An old man and a boy - no offence, Prof - in a crummy old doll factory. No way!'

Tolemy knew that it would be useless trying to explain, so he got on with filling in next week's football coupon.

'Ask me no questions and I'll tell you no lies,' said the professor mischievously.

'You always were a devious old devil, Melmo!'

'The point is, my dear Hodge, do you want to work on the project, or not?'

Hodge started to laugh. 'Try and stop me!'

'Good,' said Tolemy, folding up his coupon ready to give to Mr Hastie. 'There's no time to lose. The first materials will be delivered tomorrow.'

'Hang about,' protested Hodge. 'We need an extensive component development schedule. I can cope with the peripheral circuits, but the Central Processing Unit...'

'The CPU will not be a problem.'

'If you can afford about fifteen years solid research.'

'The first robot will be completed,' Tolemy announced with inspired confidence, 'within three weeks.'

'Well, bugger me!' said Hodge.

Inspector Cordingly arrived at the Annex to find General Spiby busy at his desk. The old soldier was building a child's model robot. His blotter was littered with the skeletal spars from which components had been stripped, together with a number of pieces for which he could find no place. Puddles of spilled, Airfix glue blistered the work surface. The inspector watched in silence as the general annointed the robot's head with another generous blob of adhesive before crowning it with a modular scanning unit. Sir Percival was now complete and could join his comrades in plastic - Sir Lancelot, Sir Gawain, Sir Kay - who stood to attention on shelves around the room.

The general's secretary had reported the old man's latest obsession to Henry Fraddon, but the civil servant had been quite unperturbed by the news. The inquiry into the PZ1 affair was going along very nicely and he was only too happy for his adversary from the Annex to be so harmlessly occupied. 'The world would be a safer and a happier place,' Fraddon observed, 'if more of our political and military leaders played with *toy* soldiers instead of the real thing.' Miss Wheeler could only agree, and continued - quite happily - running errands for the general to Hamleys Of Regent Street.

'Well, Charles? What do you think?'

The inspector looked around at the growing army of model robots, thinking that the general was ripe for the funny farm. But it would not do to mock. After all, the old boy had the right idea - however crazy it seemed at the time - about the man from the building society. Inspector Cordingly also had a bit of a soft spot for his former Tank Commander. 'Very impressive,' he muttered tactfully.

General Spiby's right hand had begun to twitch. He seized a small brush, dipped it in a jar of black paint and, with the dash of a graffiti artist, drew a savage caricature face on Sir Percival's head. Cordingly now noticed that the other robots had all been over-painted with the same cruel grimace. 'Power! Domination! Control!' growled Spiby rhythmically to himself as he inspected his cut-size troops. 'All Vardons will be eliminated!'

'What are Vardons?' asked Charles Cordingly.

'Vardons? How the hell should I know!' snapped the general, as if unaware of his previous outburst. He transfered Sir Percival to a space on the shelf beside Sir Bedevere. 'Right, Charles. What news on our friend from the building society?'

'I think you might have been on to something with Hastie, sir.'

'Damn it, of course I was on to something!'

The inspector continued with an account of his visit to Turlow. Kevin Kettle (a worthy citizen, only too anxious to help Special Branch with their inquiries) had traced the flow of Leslie Hastie's money to the account of a previously bankrupt toy factory. The computer of the Turlow Building Society had also revealed some very extraordinary purchases for a doll manufacturer.

'Where do we go from here, Charles?' demanded the general.

'We wait, sir. See what sort of game they're playing at Tinkerbell Toys.'

'Sabotage! That's what they're playing at. They planted something in that confounded hill and destroyed my prototype!'

'It's only been established that Sergeant Monk and the man, Smart, were digging...'

'Removing the evidence!'

'Perhaps. But there's nothing at that doll factory with the power to destroy your automaton.'

'So what *is* all their equipment for?'

'I've been talking to your Head of Research...' The inspector hesitated.

'Young Bidmead? Well?'

Inspector Cordingly glanced at the general's pathetic, plastic models. He thought of the cherished PZ1 project, about to be abandoned. He knew that what he was going to say would pierce General Spiby to the heart. 'It looks as if they're building a robot.'

It was a week of frenzied activity at Tinkerbell Toys. From

the day that Tolemy sent off his first requisitions on the school computer, the deliveries began at 68, Droop Street. Dispatch riders in black leather arrived on Harley Davisons with bulging, padded bags. Heavy sealed packages came in the special parcel post. Advice notes from the Heathrow Cargo Centre spewed out of the new fax machine sending Bob Love's Metro on a relentless shuttle between factory and airport. Freight was dispatched by the hour via Red Star to Turlow Station. Rare alloys were escorted by Securicor from the docks while a batch of the latest transputers shared a taxi all the way from Gwent. A succession of vans and lorries off-loaded drums of chemical compounds and cases full of struts, cables, fibres and trunking into the cluttered bay beside the canal. To collect a consignment of dedicated machine tools from Sheffield, Tolemy even had to call upon the services of his father's artic.

Tolemy's mum and dad had long since given up asking what was going on. They had been confused, at the outset, by Charlie Protheroe's original bequest. Now, they were totally baffled by the secret project at Droop Street which consumed all Tolemy's energy and time. Mrs James merely hoped that it was all above board and would cause no talk amongst the neighbours. Mr James advised Tolemy not to neglect his studies when the new term started at school. It did, however, occur to both Sylvia and Terry that the boy might eventually make some pocket money out of his derelict property - which was no more than he deserved, considering all the hours he was putting in.

But Tolemy, far from making money, was spending it hand over fist. The first million disappeared in a matter of days, but was effortlessly replaced the following Monday. The Man from the Pools had returned to Mr Hastie's bungalow in a lather of excitement. Such a win, two weeks running, was unheard of in the company. Surely, Mr Hastie could see the value, the necessity, the public duty, even, of the fullest publicity?

'No publicity!' repeated Leslie Hastie.

'Samantha Fox? Russell Harty?' pleaded the executive, envisaging a lavish scenario which might even reach the front page of the *Sun*. But to no avail.

'By the way, Gwyneth,' said Mr Hastie as he passed his winnings to Miss Powell over the counter of the Turlow Building Society. 'Who *is* Samantha Fox?'

Miss Powell laughed and pressed the buzzer to alert Mr Kettle who duly conveyed to Scotland Yard the information that a further heavy investment had been made in Tinkerbell Toys.

In the refurbished factory, special areas had been cleared and equipped to construct the various sub-units of the robot. Where, in the old days, clockwork mechanisms for the *Swiss Miss* had been assembled, Tolemy's deftest workers now put together complex servo-muscular systems. Next door, the voiceboxes for the *Little Madam* had been junked to make way for the automaton's speech synthesiser. The old die-casting room was now an orthopaedic laboratory where gleaming legs, feet, toes, fingers and numerous joints and bearings were pressed and moulded from mysterious metals and subtle plastic amalgams. The fabric workshop, which once created the economy wardrobe of the *Downee Doll*, now fashioned the outer casing of the machine man. Night and day, relays of women attacked the stubborn material, creating - to infinitely precise measurements - an inpenetrable suit of silver armour.

Professor Melmo supervised the whole operation. 'What's happening! What's happening!' he would cry, impatiently tapping his way from room to room. 'I must know what is happening!'

In the new extension, in a dust-filtered, sterile zone, Hodge supervised the creation of the delicate capacitive sensor pads and silicone nerve ganglions. Periodically the red-haired computer wizard dashed up the motorway in an old MGB to check her complex algorythms on the mainframe computer at Darlington University.

'I just don't believe it!' she announced to Tolemy, returning from one of her flying visits north. 'These recognition and movement programs should have taken a team of experts years to compile. And you just hand them over as if you found them under a gooseberry bush!'

Tolemy smiled.

'I warn you, though,' Hodge continued. 'You're building a robot without a brain, because you'll never find a Central Processor that can handle sufficient information. Nowhere on God's Earth!'

'*Under* the Earth, perhaps,' suggested Tolemy, hurrying away for another secret session on the QX 10 with the prof. 'But not *from* the Earth,' he added quietly, thinking of the casket hidden behind the shed at home.

'How are you finding Turlow, Hodge?' said Bob, by way of polite conversation as he and the Darlington Genius pored over yet another set of plans.

'Apart from being the plughole of the Universe,' said Hodge, 'I think it's very nice.'

Bob ruminated for a moment, the spit gurgling in the bowl of his pipe. 'How about an expedition to The Hoop? They have quite a good Country and Western group on Tuesday nights.'

Hodge bit into a Mars bar to hide her embarrassment. (Bob Love was the most brilliantly intuitive engineer she had ever met and she was anxious not to upset him.) 'I'd rather have a few *explanations*.' She pointed to the details of the robot's neuro-muscular synapses. 'Where does it all come from!'

Bob shook his head and rattled a couple of pennies in his right hand pocket.

'And the cash? This project is costing thousands of pounds every minute!'

'Tolemy takes it out of the building society.'

'The building society? For heaven's sake!' She looked across to where Leslie Hastie was painstakingly entering figures in one of Charlie Protheroe's old, marbled ledgers.

'It's all part of the divine plan,' said Bob Love sagaciously.

'Bugger a divine plan!' said Hodge, scurrying back to the sterile room. 'I'm a *scientist*!'

Mr Hastie looked up from his accounting. 'Why, on the money we pay that girl, does she have to go to Oxfam for all her clothes?'

Since no answer was forthcoming he returned to the world of high finance. The Man from the Pools had brought yet another huge cheque to the bungalow that very morning. 'Omar Sharif? Princess Michael of Kent?' Names had dropped like foundation stones as the gibbering young executive bid for the publicity event of the year. Mr Hastie wondered if he should tell Hodge that her salary depended on Tolemy's unique ability to predict the treble chance. Perhaps not. The poor girl was confused enough already.

Hodge was in one of her fits of puzzle and muddle when a teenage girl in dirty denim wandered unannounced into the factory. Eddie Fox had not seen Tolemy since the evening on the heath and had been very off with him the couple of times he tried to phone. Now, she found herself missing him, and, despite all her protestations to the contrary, she was curious to know what was going on at Tinkerbell Toys. It was unfortunate she should come face to face with a moody Hodge. 'What do you want!' snapped the red-haired computer expert.

'I'm a friend of Tolemy. And who, may I ask, are *you*?'

'Tolemy's busy. You'll have to make an appointment.'

'I beg your pardon!' protested Eddie, adopting the tone of voice her mother used on the phone to the gas board.

'This research establishment is not open to ordinary members of the public. If you have anything to discuss with Mr James, I suggest you telephone his secretary.' Hodge instantly wished she could bite out her tongue.

'Get stuffed!' said Eddie. 'And tell Tolemy... Oh, who cares about Tolemy! Or his silly robot!' She turned and hurried, angry and hurt, towards the canalside entrance.

Hodge reminded herself sternly that Tolemy was only a boy, barely sixteen. It was perfectly natural that he should have friends like the girl she had just been so rude to.

Tolemy, meantime (and unknown to Hodge), had solved the problem of the Central Processing Unit. He was now convinced that the robot's electronic brain was contained in the sarcophagus he had discovered at the tomb. *I am for Tolemy and Tolemy alone*. But how did the casket open? He crept out into the garden one evening while his mum and dad were safely inside the house, watching TV. In the light of his bicycle lamp, he examined the hard, oblong box. There was no sign of a join. But brute force was certainly not the answer. He remembered, only too well, the fate of the treasure hunters on the hill.

'How can I open the casket?' said Tolemy to the Man in

Black.

'When all is prepared, take the box to the Place of Power.'

'What Place of Power?' said Tolemy, stirring fitfully in his sleep.

Towards the end of the week, a large operating table was wheeled into the sterile assembly area at 68, Droop Street. From all over the factory the completed sub-units for the robot were brought into the special room. The doors were then sealed, leaving Tolemy, Bob Love, Hodge and the professor alone inside with the vital components.

All four of them put on surgical masks and gowns. Bob and Hodge stepped up to the table and placed a blade of perforated alloy – the central vertebra of the robot – on the hard, sterilised surface. Tolemy stood beside Bob and Hodge, ready to hand them more components and provide them with whatever instruments they required.

'What's happening! What's happening!' cried Professor Melmo impatiently.

'It's all going fine,' said Tolemy, describing the slow growth of the robot's skeleton.

'I'm sure I can smell dust!' Melmo was nervous and tetchy. He could see the whole perfect design of the robot in his mind and longed to be able to take a more active part in its realisation.

Tolemy understood how the blind scientist must be feeling. 'Relax, Prof,' he whispered kindly, and poured some coffee from the flask Mrs Reekie had provided.

The professor took one sip. 'Who's responsible for this disgusting brew?' he protested. 'It isn't even fit for a Kosnak to drink!'

'A Kosnak? What's a Kosnak?' said Tolemy with a tingle of apprehension.

'Don't ask me,' replied Professor Melmo, oblivious of what he had just said. But it was a word Tolemy would never forget.

Like a maturing foetus, the robot on the table slowly grew. Hodge implanted the peripheral circuits and a silicon spinal chord. Bob installed the pre-fabricated muscular units and strung the tendon rigs.

'What's happening! What's happening!' the professor repeated at intervals - otherwise keeping up a regular commentary on what the others should be doing. But his advice was hardly needed. Everything fitted miraculously together.

Outside the operating theatre, the factory was idle. But the staff refused to go home. They stood around, anxious for news from behind the closed doors of the sterile room.

By the evening, Tolemy, Hodge, Bob and the professor were exhausted. It was time to stop for the day. As the doors of the construction area were unsealed, the workers waiting in the corridor peered into the protected zone. There were gasps of amazement at the sight of the silver embryo on the operating table.

Leslie Hastie was waiting amongst the factory staff as Tolemy came through the double doors, still swathed in his surgical gown. Mr Hastie had intended telling the boy about the man in the blue Cortina who he was sure was watching the factory - who had already spent several hours spying on the bungalow in Ossington Lane. But Tolemy looked dead tired and Hastie decided to leave the matter till later.

'Hi, Leslie,' said Tolemy wearily. 'Can we borrow your old Morris tomorrow?' He gave no details of the journey for which the ancient Traveller would be required. Nor did Mr Hastie ask for any.

'You have done well, my child,' said the Man in Black. 'We shall meet no more. But I leave you with all that was and is and shall be of Vardon.'

Tolemy peered through the mist of sleep at the silver warriors who surrounded his guide. And he saw that they all were men of metal.

'Farewell, Tolemy,' said the Man in Black. *'Excelsior!'*

First thing next morning, work resumed in the sterile chamber. The robot's limbs were fitted and the scanning unit and head were fixed to the end of its torso. The power unit and gyro stabilisers were installed, then a flashing cordon of control points and activity modules was attached around its waist. The robot was virtually complete.

He lay on the table in an attitude of prayerful death like a knight from a mediaeval monument. 'That's as far as we go,' announced Hodge. 'I warned you. Without a CPU it's all a bit of a redundant exercise.' She pointed to a narrow slit in the robot's chest where the creature's brain was designed to go. Without that their creation was a mere heap of parts.

Tolemy was not dismayed. 'We must take him to the Place of Power.'

Hodge frowned. She suspected that something unscientific was afoot. 'What place of power?'

'Stonehenge, of course,' said Tolemy, starting to remove his mask and gown.

It was already dark by the time the two vehicles slipped out of the factory yard into Droop Street. Professor Melmo travelled with Hodge in her sports car while Bob Love, with Tolemy at his side, drove Mr Hastie's Morris. The robot had been placed in an open crate, like a corpse in a lidless coffin, which just fitted in the back of the old station wagon.

They soon cleared Turlow New Town and started to speed through open country. For a while, they followed each other west along the M4, then turned left onto the A34. A little more than an hour after leaving Turlow they drew up on the edge of Salisbury Plain. A hundred yards from where they were parked was the sacred circle of giant stones, erected by neolithic man over three thousand years ago.

Low, swirling cloud began to form around the henge as they transferred the heavy crate to a small trolley and trundled it across the grass to the edge of the circle. Bob Love insisted they carry no lights for fear of drawing attention to their visit, so they stumbled and blundered in the dark – except for Professor Melmo who was used to finding his way unsighted. When they reached the perimeter fence they lifted the crate off the wheels and manhandled it through the wire and over the ditch. All four of them then carried it on their shoulders, like pall-bearers, to the centre of the ring of standing stones where it was laid to rest on the ground.

'There's one thing more we need,' said Tolemy, scurrying back to the car.

'What's happening! What's happening!' cried the professor.

'Bugger all,' muttered Hodge, wondering what all the mumbo-jumbo could possibly be in aid of.

Tolemy soon came running back, carrying a small ceramic box.

'What's that?' said Bob.

'Wait and see,' said Tolemy, placing the casket - which he had earlier retrieved from his father's compost heap - on the grass beside the robot.

They stood in silence in the centre of the henge. Now that their eyes had got used to the dark they could just make out the concentric circles of giant stones which surrounded them. The little group of humans felt themselves at the heart of a terrible, brooding power.

The wind began to rise - but with no effect on the blanket of oppressive cloud that smothered the henge. Thunder rumbled around the plain.

'What's happening!' shouted the professor.

'Stand back!' cried Tolemy.

The wind whirled and screamed within the confines of the megaliths. The thunder shook the ground. Hodge, terrified, grabbed Bob Love by the arm. The professor stood with his head bowed. Tolemy stared up into the sky.

With an almighty crash, a jagged ray of blinding light burst from the cloud, shattering the sarcophagus at their feet.

Then all was quiet. The cloud had evaporated in an instant and the air was calm again. The moon shone brightly from a star-spangled sky. Tolemy suddenly felt heavy, clumsy, stupid even. Something had left him.

The professor was weeping. 'So dark. So dark.'

'Look!' Bob pointed to the ground. Amongst the shards of the broken casket, something glinted.

Tolemy knelt on the grass and picked up the contents of the box from the tomb. He showed to his companions a gleaming, silver disc. 'All that was and is and shall be of Vardon.' He moved to the crate and placed the metal wafer in the breastplate of the robot.

There was the crackle of static electricity and a fluttering sound. Within the machine flowed energy, power... and *life*!

The robot lifted his hands and pushed at the sides of the crate which splintered like matchwood. The silver creature rose to his feet, stretched out his right arm and grasped the hand of the boy beside him. 'Tolemy!' he declaimed in a low, steady voice.

'Who are you?' said Tolemy, gazing up at two great shining eyes.

'I am Drumnadrockit,' said the robot.

CHAPTER FIVE

Plastic model robots with horrid, leering faces sat around the general's office like garden gnomes in Surbiton. 'Power! Dominion! Control!' recited Spiby between clenched teeth in the manner of an amateur ventriloquist. 'All Vardons will be eliminated. Kosnaks will endure for ever!'

Henry Fraddon placed a thick folder marked *Top Secret* on the general's desk. 'The Report on PZ1. Not an optimistic prognosis, I fear, General.'

General Spiby thrust the document aside and picked up a neutron blaster (Miss Wheeler's latest acquisition from the toy shop). 'Zap! Zap! Zap! You're a dead man, Fraddon!'

The civil servant laughed. Already, he could hear the tumbrils carting away the loony occupants of the Annex. He could afford to be generous with his old opponent. 'I do like your little ornaments, Arthur.' He looked round at the miniaturised automata. 'You've made the office positively pretty.'

The general growled quietly. As soon as Fraddon had left he picked up the phone and called Scotland Yard. 'Charles? Spiby! We're going in. I must know what they're up to at that damned doll factory!'

It was nearly midnight by the time the contingent from Tinkerbell Toys left the stone circle at Stonehenge. Hodge and the professor, both reluctant to be parted from their amazing progeny, went home in the MG. Tolemy travelled in the back of the Morris, with Drumnadrockit sitting in the front on account of his long legs.

'Where did your brain come from?' Tolemy asked his new companion. 'The CPU? And all that information?'

'From Vardon,' exclaimed Drumnadrockit.

'Vardon?' said Bob, driving steadily up the centre lane of the motorway. 'That's a new one on me. Somewhere in South America, is it?'

'In the Constellation of Orion,' Drumnadrockit corrected him.

'Is that a fact?' Bob chewed ruminatively on the stem of his pipe. He hadn't bargained on the divine plan involving intelligences from Outer Space. He wasn't sure he liked the idea of that at all.

'Of course, strictly speaking, Vardon *isn't*,' continued the robot. 'We were wiped out in a cataclysmic war.' He shifted in the passenger seat like an arthritic granny.

'Anything wrong?' said Tolemy anxiously.

'Mustn't grumble,' said Drumnadrockit philosophically. 'You all did remarkably well, considering your primitive technology.'

There was a dull thud, and Mr Hastie's old jalopy veered sharply to the left. 'Puncture!' cursed Bob, steering the station wagon on to the hard shoulder. To their amazement the vehicle carried a spare wheel in tolerable condition. There was, however, no sign of a jack. 'Thank you, Leslie!' muttered Bob Love, wondering what would happen if a passing patrol car spotted their silver passenger.

The Morris suddenly tilted to the right, raising the flat tyre clear of the ground. 'Get a move on, Bob!' came a voice from the nearside. Drumnadrockit had got out of his seat and stood beside the vehicle. One metal hand was extended underneath the jack point, the other was clasped around the rusted nuts of the offending wheel. Within a minute they were back on the motorway, approaching the Turlow exit.

Tolemy yawned. 'You are tired', observed Drumnadrockit. 'Leave me at the factory. Then go home and get some rest.'

Tolemy readily agreed, looking forward to a dreamless sleep. He knew there would be no more visitations from the

Man in Black; and no more intuitions. He was an ordinary boy again (what a relief!). The spirit of Vardon now resided in the silver robot he had created, together, Tolemy suspected, with numerous remarkable talents.

Inspector Cordingly and Derek Bidmead entered the Droop Street premises just before dawn. The inspector was quite accustomed to breaking into property without benefit of a search warrant, though Spiby's Head of Research felt decidedly less comfortable.

'Well?' said Cordingly as the scientist examined the equipment in the assembly area.

'This is all consistent with the computer data from the building society.'

'Any sign of an end product?'

'I'm not sure...'

Something moved outside in the corridor. Cordingly grabbed Derek Bidmead and dragged him behind the door. 'Must be a nightwatchman,' he whispered.

Someone - or some*thing* - entered the room. In the dim light, the two men behind the door could just discern a vague shadow. The shadow turned towards them. Out of the darkness two, large, glowing, red eyes peered at the intruders. 'There is no need to hide, Inspector Cordingly,' came a faintly disembodied voice. 'Doctor Bidmead, do please come away from the door.'

Both men froze.

'Perhaps one of you gentlemen could provide some illumination,' the speaker continued politely.

The inspector found a switch beside the door and turned on the light to reveal a robot standing in the centre of the room. 'A fair cop, as you say at Scotland Yard, Inspector,' said Drumnadrockit.

The uninvited visitors were dumbfounded.

The robot took a few steps towards them. 'I take it you don't have any authority for this intrusion?'

Derek Bidmead, all his previous fear forgotten, was now trembling with excitement. 'It walks! It talks! It's amazing!' he stammered, thinking of his own disastrous experiments in robotics.

'It? It?' protested Drumnadrockit. 'I'm not the cat, you

know!'

'Artificial intelligence *and* a programmed personality!' cried the scientist.

'Programmed nothing!' the robot interrupted. 'I think, therefore I am!'

Inspector Cordingly swore quietly to himself never to laugh at Spiby again. 'How did you know our names?' he asked the silver creature, trying hard not to lose his professional cool.

'My dear fellow, I know *all* about you. And your friend from Special Projects.' Drumnadrockit raised a reptilian finger to the crew-cut mesh on the top of his head. 'My psycho-sensor units. Now, if you will excuse me . . .' He led them out into the corridor. 'I have a lot of work to do before the factory re-opens in the morning.'

The two men followed obediently.

'As you see,' continued Drumnadrockit, shepherding them towards the main entrance, 'everything ship-shape and Bristol fashion. Nothing to concern Special Branch.' He opened the door and deposited two very confused humans on the pavement of Droop Street.

The Right Honourable Justin Watkin stared at the report on his desk. He said nothing, but drummed with his fingers on the green leather surface. Henry Fraddon stood at his side, the merest smile on his face, thinking how easier life was going to be once the Annex had been closed down. Big Ben began to strike ten o'clock. Justin Watkin slowly closed the file and placed it in his red dispatch box.

'Well, Minister?'

'You know a female person' – there was a bitter tone to Watkin's voice – 'called Charity O'Toole?'

'Certainly, Minister. American Liason. Ms O'Toole attended the trials on Turlow Heath . . .'

'Quite, quite.' The Minister was silent again, rubbing his chin as he gazed out on the distant prospect of Horse Guards Parade. 'Your Mizz O'Toole,' he continued, 'has put it about the Pentagon that Her Majesty's Government has as much chance of achieving a successful robotics programme as it has of breeding pigs to fly the Atlantic!'

'Indeed?' Henry Fraddon, who had been spreading the

same story around Whitehall, pretended to look shocked.

'The Americans are *reconsidering* some rather valuable Star Wars sub-contracts which would otherwise have gone to British companies. I need hardly say that the Prime Minister is not best pleased.'

Poor Henry Fraddon's mind was in a whirl as he struggled to think of a scheme of damage limitation.

But the Minister took the initiative. 'I think we should consider this document as an essentially *interim* assessment,' he announced, closing the dispatch box. 'In the meantime, I understand there may have been some interesting developments in this line of technology ... in the private sector.' He glanced again at the note he had just received from General Spiby.

'The private sector?' repeated the civil servant, appalled.

'I think it's time we got our act together,' said the minister. 'A successful robotics programme could hold the key to the future prosperity and security of our country.'

'I do so agree,' echoed Henry Fraddon frigidly.

'Knights in shining armour. A new Arthurian age...'

'If you will excuse me, Minister.' Henry Fraddon hurried from the room. He was rather afraid he was going to be sick.

Both Tolemy and the professor arrived late at the factory where the staff had been given the day off on account of all their hard work and overtime building the robot. There was no sign of Drumnadrockit where they had left him in the assembly area. Someone, however, was at work in the portacabin office. It was Hodge, desperately trying to access data from the computer.

'Everything's been erased!' she cried distraughtly as Tolemy came in with the professor. 'All your research destroyed. Even the back-up disks are blank!'

Suddenly the office was filled with the delicate aroma of fresh coffee as Drumnadrockit came into the portacabin with a steaming jug and three cups on a tray. 'I trust this will be to your liking, Professor,' said the robot.

For a moment, Hodge completely forgot about the missing data and gazed in wonder at their silver prodigy. Drumnadrockit stared back at the computer expert with his soulful red eyes. 'The information has been removed,' he announced, reading her mind. 'It was *necessary*.' He poured a cup of coffee and gently placed it in the professor's hand.

'I... wish... to... retrieve... data,' said Hodge to the robot as if talking to a deaf aunt down a bad telephone line.

'My dear girl,' replied Drumnadrockit, 'there's no need to speak as if I were a half-wit. My audio-vocal systems are as good as yours, if not better.' His bright eyes seemed, for a moment, to twinkle mischievously. 'As for the data, as I have already explained, it has been tranferred to my own infinitely superior memory systems.'

Hodge immediately felt less reverential towards their new creation. 'You wilfully destroyed our computer files?' she shouted angrily.

'The information is all in my matrix and can be made available at my discretion.'

'Well done, Drumnadrockit,' murmured the professor sipping his coffee. 'First decent cup I've had in this place.'

'Let's get something straight,' protested Hodge. 'Like, who's the monkey and who's the organ grinder. We *created* you!'

'I think you're being a little presumptuous, my dear,' replied Drumnadrockit. 'You're not God, you know.'

To prevent Hodge having a heart attack, Tolemy tried to explain about Vardon.

'Pull the other one, Tolemy!'

'It's perfectly simple,' said Drumnadrockit. 'My matrix contains the memory and knowledge of a long-dead people - people from another world.'

'Well, bugger me!' said Hodge. She stared at the robot, appalled. Too late, she realised what they had done. At the behest of an alien intelligence they had created a new Frankenstein's monster with infinite knowledge of the Universe, whose motives...

'There is no need to be alarmed, my dear,' Drumnadrockit interrupted Hodge's racing thoughts. 'You will find the ideals and the culture of Vardon entirely compatible with your own best instincts. Our knowledge and experience is to be used for the benefit and security of Earth.'

'Why *Earth*?' Tolemy asked very seriously.

'We have been in contact with your planet for many centuries.'

'Not that garbage of Leslie Hastie!' interrupted Hodge. 'Spacemen and prehistoric man...'

Drumnadrockit suddenly stiffened. He held up a silver hand. 'Outsiders!' he warned.

General Spiby got out of the car and looked around the poky little yard of 68, Droop Street. So this was where the pestiferous Hastie had been operating from. 'Enemy territory,' he whispered to Derek Bidmead.

'General, I don't think you quite understand the situation,' replied the Head of Research. 'These people can hardly be considered our competitors. Their machine is a quantum leap beyond our own robotic development.'

'We'll see about that,' growled the general, tapping peremptorily on the window of the limousine where Henry Fraddon sat sulking.

'Well, gents?' said Tolemy as Bob Love escorted the party from Whitehall into the portacabin office. 'What can we do for you?'

The general had no intention of discussing matters with a mere office boy. 'Who's in charge!' he bellowed.

'I am,' said Tolemy.

'Bless my soul,' said General Spiby.

'These are my colleagues. Hodge, Professor Melmo...'

'Melmo!' cried Henry Fraddon, spotting his old irritant from the Annex. 'Is this another of your madcap schemes?'

'Mind your own business,' snapped the professor, recognising the weasel voice of the mandarin.

'Gentlemen, please,' protested the general. He turned to the civil servant. 'Get on with it, Fraddon.'

It nauseated Henry Fraddon to go cap in hand to the likes of Melmo and his weirdo friends. 'There is a remote possibility,' he announced, staring sullenly at a filing cabinet, 'that some of your research may be of peripheral interest to Her Majesty's Government.'

'Bugger Her Majesty's Government,' shouted Hodge.

'We are engaged on a peaceful, private project,' explained Bob Love reasonably, shaking his pipe into the waste paper basket.

General Spiby began to murmur quietly to himself. 'Kosnaks will dominate. All Vardons will be destroyed...'

'What did you say!' cried Tolemy, wondering whether he'd heard the old soldier correctly.

There was a knock at the half-open door and the silver figure of Drumnadrockit strode into the room. 'Perhaps you gentlemen would care for some refreshment,' he announced urbanely. 'Coffee? Or perhaps a whisky and soda, eh, General?'

Spiby and Fraddon stared open-mouthed at the gleaming automaton.

'What did I tell you!' said Derek Bidmead excitedly to his colleagues.

Tolemy and Hodge looked at each other and grinned.

'What's happening! What's happening!' grumbled the professor.

'Our friends from London have a temporary credibility problem,' Drumnadrockit explained obligingly.

General Spiby continued to gaze at the robot as if in the throes of a religious experience. 'A knight in shining armour!' he gasped. 'Sir Galahad himself!'

'My name is Drumnadrockit if it's all the same to you,' the metal man corrected him.

Henry Fraddon reappraised the situation with the speed of light. This Droop Street robot was in a far different league from Derek Bidmead's heap of junk. With a machine like Drumnadrockit on their side he could soon tell that O'Toole woman where to get off. 'The work you have done here,' he explained patronisingly to Tolemy, 'could be of great national importance.'

'What's that supposed to mean?' interrupted Drumnadrockit suspiciously.

'Your country needs you!' bawled the general.

Drumnadrockit raised a testudinous hand. 'That is for Tolemy to decide.'

All eyes were upon Tolemy as he remained silent for a good minute. 'Our work here,' he finally announced in a slow, wise voice, 'is for the benefit of the entire human race. Not for the advantage of individual governments. I'm sorry, gentlemen, but you seem to have had a wasted journey.'

They watched from the window as the black car reversed out into Droop Street and sped off in the direction of the motorway. Drumnadrockit stood rigidly to attention, his head slightly back. A faint but sinister purring sound came from his sensor units. 'Something is wrong!' declared the robot. 'Did you not feel it?'

'Feel what, Drumnadrockit?'

The mechanical emissary of Vardon lowered his head and turned to face his human creators. 'Great danger!'

Eddie Fox sat by the phone at *Westaways* in an agony of indecision. Six times she had dialled the factory at Droop Street, only to bang down the receiver before the bell could ring. It was now three weeks since her encounter with Hodge. (Hodge, indeed - more like a *hedge* in Eddie's opinion!) Why hadn't Tolemy rung her? She would have refused to have talked to him, of course, but at least contact would have been re-established.

It was her mother's suggestion that Tolemy go with them that evening to *The Sound Of Music* in the school hall...

The phone rang in the portacabin. 'Oh, hi, Eddie.' Tolemy felt a pang of guilt. He'd been meaning to call Edwina for ages. 'Tonight? Well, I'll *try*...'

'Tonight,' said Drumnadrockit to Mr Hastie whom he had summoned to attend him in the assembly area of Tinkerbell Toys. 'As soon as it is dark. We shall require your vehicle.'

'The old Morris? Okey-doke.' Mr Hastie was looking forward to a good long talk with the robot. 'Those points of the Decagon,' he began. 'The sacred sites...?'

'Energy control centres,' explained the robot. 'Vardon generators are concealed in the ground all over your planet.'

'Orgone power!' cried Hastie triumphantly. 'We'll show those know-all scientists a thing or two!'

'All will be revealed tonight,' said Drumnadrockit.

'Can't it wait till tomorrow?' protested Tolemy who had just decided that a few hours away from the factory with

Eddie and her mum was just what the doctor ordered.

'There is no time to waste,' warned the Vardon robot. 'Defensive measures must be taken for the protection of Earth.'

'Whoever has power over that robot,' said the general to his companions in the black Rover as they hurried up the motorway towards London, 'has power over the world.'

Fraddon stared ahead through the windscreen like a zombie. He was a changed man. Droop Street had been his Damascus Road. Though the general did not yet realise it, Henry Fraddon had just become his most devoted disciple.

'A few of those things in Belfast,' continued the general, 'and we can sort out the Irish in a week. Patrols in the inner cities, in the coloured ghettos and the vandalised housing estates . . .' His vision of a Britain, proud, safe and secure came suddenly into hard focus. His travelling companions murmured their agreement.

It did not occur to any of them to take Tolemy's refusal to co-operate with the Ministry seriously. They wanted the power of the robot from the toy factory. And they would have it.

'First right, second left, straight on,' instructed Drumnadrockit from the front passenger seat of Mr Hastie's Morris. It seemed an odd way to a Vardon Control Centre – across Turlow and into the Old Town . . . 'Turn in here, please, and stop,' the robot ordered.

'What's this for?' asked Tolemy as Leslie Hastie brought the station wagon to a halt under the monkey puzzle tree of *Westaways*.

'You wish to see your friend.' Drumnadrockit's eyes definitely twinkled. 'We will continue with our work when you have explained the situation to the young lady.'

Tolemy grinned. Drumnadrockit had read his mind precisely.

Mr Fox (who would have nothing to do with Philip Attwood's antics in the school hall) had just settled down with a bottle of his favourite Isle of Mull whisky for an illicit hour of *Dallas* when the doorbell rang. Quickly switching over to the news on Channel Four, he went out into the hall and opened the front door. 'Why, Tolemy!'

'Mr Fox... Bernard, can I have a word with Eddie?'

'Just missed her. I'm afraid. Look, come in for a moment...' Mr Fox steered Tolemy into the sitting room. It was about time somebody explained what was going on between the boy and his daughter, and what had happened that night on Turlow Heath. (It was no good asking Edwina or her mother.) 'You two had a row?' he asked bluntly.

'No!' protested Tolemy. 'I was just tied up at the factory and... Bernard, I've got to go.'

Mr Fox was not convinced. 'You can talk frankly to me, old chap. I'm pretty broad-minded, you know.' The left side of Mr Fox's face twitched ludicrously as he attempted a wink.

'Mr... Bernard...' Tolemy blushed scarlet. 'She was only jealous...'

'Another girlfriend?'

'I mean jealous about the robot.'

'Your meccano man? How's that coming along by the way?'

'Not bad,' said Tolemy, glad to change the subject.

'I'd like to see what you've done. Give you a few tips, perhaps.'

Mr Fox's wish was instantly fulfilled. There was a heavy footstep in the hall, the door opened and Drumnadrockit joined them. 'We ought to be getting a move on, Tolemy,' said the robot.

There was a strangled hiccup from Bernard Fox. His mouth popped open like a pedal bin.

'Drumnadrockit, Mr Fox. Bernard, this is my robot.' Tolemy made the introductions.

'How do you do, Mr Fox,' said Drumnadrockit raising a metal hand.

Mr Fox's right arm slowly levitated. As the schoolmaster's fingers touched the cold, hard scales of his visitor he wondered whether he was dreaming or had taken too much vintage Whisper of Mull.

'I won't be a moment. Go and tell Leslie to turn the car, please, Drumnadrockit,' ordered Tolemy.

'Very good,' intoned Drumnadrockit. He nodded stiffly

to Mr Fox and marched out of the room. Unseen by the humans, the robot paused in the hall, reassessing the data in his electronic brain. His red eyes scanned the Foxes' hat stand. Then, grabbing an overcoat, a scarf and a tweed trilby he continued to the still-open front door. Drumnadrockit halted again on the doorstep. On the far side of the drive was another vehicle, infinitely more capacious than Mr Hastie's and far better suited to the business in hand...

'Well, what do you think?' Tolemy lingered in the sitting room, thoroughly enjoying Bernard Fox's consternation.

'Most impressive,' stammered Mr Fox. 'I...' He was interrupted by the roar of a powerful engine in the front drive. 'My God!' he yelled, rushing to the window. 'Some bastard's gone and pinched the Volvo!'

'Don't blame me,' complained Mr Hastie, desperately trying to keep up with Bernard Fox's stolen hatchback as they careered round the roundabout on the edge of the bypass. 'That coat and hat. I thought it was Mr Fox.'

'Now where's he gone?' cried Tolemy, trying to peer round a large Telecom van that had swerved in front of them.

'It's no good,' said Leslie, turning off towards the New Town Centre. 'We've lost him.'

Drumnadrockit's self-programming systems soon got the hang of the primitive Earth vehicle. It was all quite simple, really. A crude explosive device transmitted energy through a variable reduction unit... He rounded a corner of the open road into the glaring lights of another vehicle on collision course. He quickly entered new data: drive on the left! Drumnadrockit tugged at the steering wheel and Mr Fox's Volvo swerved to the nearside, missing, by inches, the approaching police car.

'Bleedin' Ada!' PC Tom Rivers braked violently.

'Z Victor Three to Control...' Constable Barnfather in the passenger seat picked up the radio to check the number of the offending vehicle while Constable Rivers backed the police car into the gate of a field. 'Let's get after the crazy sod!'

Their pursuit was not as swift as it might have been. A fat, holiday caravan came round the bend, hogging the road and leading a half-mile tailback of frustrated motorists and their cars. Lights flashing and siren wailing, the patrol car dodged in and out of the crawling column, but, by the time it overtook the swaying mobile home, there was no sign of the Volvo.

'Keep going, Tom,' Keith Barnfather peered ahead.

'Control to Z Victor Three,' crackled the radio. 'Green Volvo, registered owner Bernard Francis Fox. Reported stolen . . .'

'Look!' They both spotted the Volvo ahead in a layby alongside a large field. Tom Rivers cut the siren, light, and engine, and they coasted silently into the verge about fifty yards behind Mr Fox's missing car.

There was no sign of any driver as they walked round the abandoned vehicle. But in the centre of the adjoining field they could just make out the shape of a man in an overcoat and trilby striding steadily into the distance. 'Where's he gone now?' muttered Tom Rivers as the figure appeared to descend into the solid earth.

'Trick of the light. He'll be back,' observed PC Barnfather confidently as the two police officers settled down to wait.

It was not long before the mystery man reappeared, his arms full of bundles and crates. 'What's the betting that stuff's nicked and all?' whispered Tom Rivers, thinking happily of the commendation ahead from Superintendent Bellis.

'Must have the muscles of a fork-lift truck!' remarked Keith Barnfather a trifle nervously as the overcoated figure trundled steadily across the field and up to the back of the parked vehicle.

'Excuse me, sir,' said PC Rivers, stepping out of the shadows. 'Police officers. Would you mind showing us . . .' The words froze on the constable's lips as the 'man' turned slowly towards them. Under the open overcoat was a body of hard silver; beneath the jaunty hat, a head of tin. Two glassy cat's-eyes reflected an ominous red back from the alien face towards the officers of the law. Before the terrified men had time to move, the metal monster had taken a black tube from the belt at his waist. The humans were surrounded by a throbbing, golden glow. With the merest grunt, they slumped to the roadside.

'Climb every mountain,' warbled Sister Maria (alias Gwyneth Powell of the Turlow Building Society), 'Ford every stream...'

'What's happened to the Abominable Hedge Woman?' whispered Eddie Fox, leaning across her mother to the seat where Tolemy had installed himself after the second interval of *The Sound Of Music*. 'And where's Smellie Leslie?'

'Do be quiet, Edwina!' hissed Mrs Fox.

Tolemy sat back in his chair and closed his eyes. It had been a hideous evening. There was no knowing where Drumnadrockit had got to with Mr Fox's car. He only hoped the robot would make it back home to Droop Street without starting World War Three.

'Where's your robot, then?' continued Eddie unkindly to a chorus of protests from the row behind.

'Really, Edwina!' muttered Mrs Fox.

It had been a mistake, Tolemy decided, coming to the hall. But there had been no point in searching the country at random for Drumnadrockit. And it had seemed an opportunity to mend his fences with Eddie. Some chance of that!

'Follow every rainbow till you find your dream!' caterwauled Turlow New Town's Julie Andrews.

Seated in his cubicle, Mr Scragg the caretaker saw a car pull into the car park and stop. Someone was a bit late for the show. He peered through the glass. Looked like Mr Fox...

Philip Attwood's peevish baritone now enthralled the occupants of the school hall. 'Edelweiss, Edelweiss,' he bleated bravely.

Tolemy was fast asleep. He came to with a start as a door at the back of the hall opened. 'Tolemy!' fluted a delicate little voice.

'Shh!' went the row behind.

In the dim light at the rear of the auditorium, Tolemy could just discern the shadow of a man. He appeared to be wearing an overcoat and a trilby hat. Tolemy's heart tumbled to his boots.

'Edelweiss, Edelweiss,' serenaded the *lederhosen* headmaster from the stage.

'Tolemy!' repeated a voice of curiously melodic timbre from the rear.

There was a disgruntled murmuring from the audience in the back seats.

'Trust Tolemy to cause a disturbance,' sniffed Edwina Fox spitefully. 'And which of your grubby friends is this?'

'Edelweiss, small and bright,' hooted the head as he strode around his cardboard mountain top. 'Bless my homeland for ever.'

The large person in the overcoat started to perambulate down the central aisle. Tolemy slid low in his seat and pretended he wasn't there. The latecomer drew level with the Foxes and their guest. *Go away, Drumnadrockit!* willed Tolemy silently. *Please!*

The disguised robot stood still. There was a whirring sound from his psycho-sensor units.

'Oh, God,' said a woman in the row behind (who had assumed the intruder to be a drunk). 'He's going to be sick!'

Drumnadrockit was obviously aware of the presence of his master but made no further move to approach the boy. Either he had heard Tolemy's frantic prayer, or... Tolemy dared a furtive glance to his left. The robot stood beside him in the gangway, his eyes riveted on the colourful pageant ahead.

'Edelweiss, Edelweiss,' yodeled Mr Attwood.

There came a plaintif echo, as if the vocal line had been reprised by a distant Wurlitzer. Heads turned.

'Edelweiss small and bright,' piped the amateur Von Trapp defiantly from the stage.

'Edelweiss small and bright!' trumpeted the voice in the body of the hall.

Some of the less culturally-minded members of the audience (whose bottoms had been pressed against the hard school chairs for the best part of three hours) began to laugh. Mrs Courtney-Hocking, the Musical Director, frantically signalled the orchestra to play more loudly.

'Edelweiss, small and bright...' belted out the headmaster.

'Bless my homeland for ever,' parodied Drumnadrockit

in a confident diapason and began to amble purposefully towards the stage.

'That man's wearing Bernard's overcoat and the fishing hat we bought last year in Betws-y-Coed!' expostulated Mrs Fox.

The robot strode forward, his unbuttoned coat parting like a flasher's mac to reveal a bright, naked body. The spectators in the front row screamed. The song froze on Philip Attwood's lips as he caught sight of the glaring red eyes under Mr Fox's cheeky tweed hat. The accompaniment ran down like a gramophone record as the orchestra – seeing the man of metal looming over them – scattered in a welter of black bombazine.

Drumnadrockit now sang on alone with full harmony backing from his own vocal synthesiser. 'Edelweiss, Edelweiss . . .' The entire Family Von Trapp abandoned their tuneful progress to Switzerland in favour of a quick flight into the wings as the singing robot sprang onto the stage. 'Small and white . . .' To steady himself, Drumnadrockit grabbed at a painted backdrop of the Alps which avalanched downwards to reveal a chorus of terrified nuns.

The audience now began to applaud what was becoming the most dynamic production of the Turlow Amateur Operatic Society in living memory.

'Philistines! Vandals!' wailed Mr Attwood as he tried to calm a writhing and hysterical Mother Superior.

Tolemy stared at the stage with a mixture of fascination and terror that he had not experienced since the forest fire in *Bambi*. It was clear that, since his lone visit to the Vardon Control Centre, Drumnadrockit had become more flexible, versatile – and dangerously independent. He also gave every appearance of actively *enjoying* himself! Tolemy suddenly remembered the details of one of Professor Melmo's blueprints. 'Excuse me . . .' He pushed past the Foxes and hurried towards the stage door.

'Is there a doctor in the house?' shouted Kevin Kettle in his capacity as Stage Manager (a pregnant novice had just gone into premature labour).

Drumnadrockit, holding the centre of the stage, began slowly to revolve, the lights on the control band round his waist fizzing like a firework display. 'Vardon! Vardon!' he chanted as if it were a football team.

Forcing his way through four of Mr Attwood's weeping stage children, Tolemy emerged behind the proscenium arch. 'Drumnadrockit! Stop it at once!' he scolded severely.

'But I'm *happy,*' protested Drumnadrockit.

'Nonsense,' said Tolemy, fumbling under Mr Fox's overcoat and between the creature's shoulders as if for the catch of a brastrap. 'Robots don't have feelings.'

'Well *I* do, and *I'm* a ro . . .' Drumnadrockit froze in mid syllogism as Tolemy found the emergency power cut-off – and Kevin Kettle rang down the curtain.

Constable Rivers and Constable Barnfather woke up feeling cold and wet – which was not surprising as they were both lying in a ditch. They could remember nothing of what had happened in the last few hours except for the dazzling headlights of an oncoming vehicle.

As they stumbled stiffly towards their abandoned patrol car, the radio crackled into life. 'Control to Z Victor Three. Go to Turlow Comprehensive School. Caretaker reports a disturbance in the hall . . .'

Henry Fraddon, with a complacent smile, dumped a pile of technical drawings on General Spiby's desk. 'From Tinkerbell Toys. We had all the plans and computer files copied last night.'

The general nodded cautiously. It was a novel and unnerving experience to have Fraddon's active co-operation. 'How did your people cope with the silver knight?'

'The robot was not on the premises.' The civil servant moved to a large wall map of the UK. 'I've arranged to re-equip the workshops on the old aerodrome at RAF Tregolls. ' He pointed to the north coast of Cornwall.

'Bit out in the sticks?'

'Security. There's a fully operational runway so we can airlift equipment and personnel. And American liason won't have to go through Heathrow.' Fraddon smiled again. He'd just had a most satisfying conversation with a rather sleepy Charity O'Toole (how remiss of him not to remember it was only 5am in the US of A). He also noted that the general had cleared away his plastic models.

There was a knock at the door and Derek Bidmead joined them.

'Well, young Bidmead. We've got the plans!'

'Some of them.'

The general turned suspiciously to Fraddon.

'It's good stuff,' the scientist quickly apologised for any apparent ingratitude. 'I'm not complaining.'

'I should hope not indeed,' said Fraddon, thinking of the hard night's burgling by Department sleuths.

'But there's no data on the peripheral control systems, or the CPU.'

'Might have known!'

'Don't worry,' said Henry Fraddon, already plotting the next move. 'I shall enjoy twisting Professor's Melmo's arm.' His face glazed over with pleasure as he reviewed the devious manoeuvres ahead. 'I'm sure we can persuade our friends at Tinkerbell Toys to play the game.' A most peculiar glottal convulsion took control of Fraddon's throat and he proceeded to squawk like a budgerigar with whooping cough. The civil servant was actually laughing.

CHAPTER SIX

Professor Melmo was busy making himself a breakfast of scrambled eggs in his microwave oven when he heard the sound of a Fiesta pulling up outside the cottage.

'I trust you are well, Professor?' said Henry Fraddon as the blind scientist opened the door.

'What do *you* want?'

'About your work at Tinkerbell Toys,' said Fraddon as the two men were seated once more beside the empty fireplace in the sitting room.

'A little retirement hobby.' Melmo smiled complacently.

'Did you ask the Ministry for permission?'

'I'm a free agent now,' said the professor unconcerned.

'Official Secrets Act, section two. Professor, I don't think you realise the seriousness . . .'

The professor laughed. 'Go and tell Spiby that there is nothing I can tell him about my robotic research . . . Even if I wanted to!'

The professor was not able to observe the hard, pinched look on Fraddon's face as he lifted a heavy file from his briefcase. 'There are a few matters that were never cleared up concerning the accident at Duncaston. And in view of certain political opinions you have made known over the years . . .'

The professor yawned. 'Sorry, but I can't concentrate without a good breakfast.'

'Unless you co-operate, the Department will make life extremely difficult for you, Professor Melmo.'

The professor smiled. 'My life is now of no significance whatsoever. Everything has been achieved.' He got slowly to his feet and fumbled for the door. 'Neither you nor the Department can hurt me any more!'

Fraddon stared, puzzled, at the scientist. This was not the same man he had so easily bullied on his previous visit.

There was a loud purring as Professor Melmo returned to the kitchen, having shown his visitor out.

'Power, greed, ambition, it's all so pointless, Pythagoras.'

Pythagoras swallowed the last piece of egg and inclined his head in a quizzical look.

'What fools they all are!'

Pythagoras turned back to the plate and started licking the butter off the toast.

'I knew no good would come of it,' said Terry James. 'I mean, why should a perfect stranger give the boy a toy factory?'

'Mind you,' said Mrs James. 'He's been a changed lad since. If you ask me, it's Tolemy who's become the stranger.' She glanced nervously at her watch. She was going to be late clocking on at Woolworths.

'Don't worry,' said Henry Fraddon. 'I'm sure nothing improper has occurred. It's just that we need certain information for our records.'

He refused another cup of instant coffee, packed up his briefcase and walked with Terry James out to the car. He sat for a moment inside his Fiesta, thinking. He was sure, now, that the boy was being used. Even Melmo, he suspected, was merely a tool. Somewhere behind the organisation of Tinkerbell Toys was a Mister Big.

The factory floor was littered with alien paraphernalia. 'What's all this, then?' It was the morning after the night before and Tolemy was not amused. He'd had the devil's own job extracting Drumnadrockit from the fracas in the school hall and providing Mr Attwood with some sort of explanation. (The headmaster was finally persuaded that it was all a practical joke by rowdies from the Polytechnic and was at that moment writing a blistering letter of complaint to the principal.) It had proved impossible, however, to mollify the Foxes and a state of severe cold war now existed between *Westaways* and 68, Droop Street.

'We need these materials,' announced Drumnadrockit, surveying the alien hoard. 'I have collected them from the bunker at the Control Centre.'

'In Mr Fox's car. Don't ever do anything like that again!'

'It was necessary.'

'It was *wrong*.'

'Robots are not programmed to make moral judgements,' said Drumnadrockit deviously. His eyes flickered and Tolemy couldn't help smiling. 'I'm sorry about my little bit of mischief,' the robot added contritely. 'I had installed some extra units into my system controls. I got rather carried away.'

Hodge had now arrived with Bob Love and was examining the mysterious hardware from the Vardon Control Centre. It was an awesome thought that the components Drumnadrockit had brought to the factory the previous evening had been hidden on Earth over a thousand years before, by travellers from another planet.

'Vardon materials are more suited to our work than the artifacts of Earth,' explained the robot.

'What work?' said Bob Love rather abruptly. He was far from happy with Drumnadrockit's trans-galactic credentials. How could they be sure that the alien representative wasn't a fifth columnist, paving the way for an invasion of little green men? Before you could say Enoch Powell there'd be Martians in Turlow taking over every fish and chip shop.

'It is necessary to construct an improved cyber unit,' Drumnadrockit explained. 'I don't want to seem ungrateful, but your technology still leaves a lot to be desired.'

'You mean build another robot?'

'If you wish. Or I can merely transfer the contents of my matrix to the new host.'

Tolemy looked across at Bob. He, too, was worried about the robot's growing independence. 'I think one of you is quite enough to be going on with.'

Hodge was far more interested in the Vardon technology. 'How could anyone make such complex circuits so *small*!' she asked the robot.

'Bio-electrolytic cloning,' explained Drumnadrockit, sorting through the cargo of parts he had brought to the factory in the back of Bernard Fox's Volvo. 'An organic paradigm of a non-organic format.'

'Your computer circuits are grown like the cells of a living brain?'

'Something like that,' said Drumnadrockit vaguely.

'Well, bugger me!' said Hodge.

'Now there's a fine upstanding chap,' exclaimed Mr Liversage as he entered the assembly area with a group of curious factory workers returning from their day off.

'There is more work on me yet to be done,' cried Drumnadrockit as the staff of Tinkerbell Toys gazed in wonder at their marvellous mannekin. 'My potential must be optimised.'

'But why?' demanded Bob Love uneasily, beginning to fear what might become of the machine they had created.

'You *need* me,' said Drumnadrockit ominously. 'There is great danger to this planet. I can help you. Together, we must be prepared...'

'Like the girl guides?' suggested Miss Tumber from the frocks department who had put on her reading glasses and was giving Drumnadrockit the once-over as if he were a hoover in Rumbelows.

'To fight the forces of evil,' said Drumnadrockit gravely.

'Sounds political to me,' muttered old Ralph Wilton from packing as he licked another roll-up.

'We are above mere politics,' insisted the robot. 'Our allegiance is to the forces of pure good.'

'Six of one and half a dozen of the other if you ask me,' observed Mrs Reekie dourly.

'There is nothing relative about evil,' answered Drumnadrockit severely.

'I'm not sure we want to be told what's what by a robot,' interrupted Mr Liversage who, like Bob Love, suspected their tin man was getting too big for his boots. 'Nothing personal,' he added, in case he might have hurt the creature's feelings.

'There is nothing to be afraid of,' Drumnadrockit reassured them. 'I am your servant not your master. And I am to be guided in all things by Tolemy.'

'Why *me*?' cried Tolemy James.

*

'Tell me about Tolemy James,' said Henry Fraddon to Mr Attwood as they sat alone in the headmaster's office at Turlow Comprehensive School.

'Remarkable boy,' said Mr Attwood, rubbing his hands together as if they were sticks with which he hoped to light a fire. 'Talented, imaginative. We have high hopes of young James. University, even.'

The headmaster found himself unable to look Fraddon in the eye and concentrated his gaze on the distant prospect of the Tesco multi-storey car park which loomed beyond the football field. The young man in question had, of course, been exonerated over *The Sound Of Music* débâcle. But there was something about Tolemy of late – a certain presence, a *knowingness* – that disturbed and embarrassed the headmaster. 'Perhaps you'd like to see the new physics laboratory, Mr Fraddon?'

'No, thank you,' said Fraddon. 'My only interest in Turlow School is Tolemy James.'

Mr Attwood had a bright idea. 'Why don't you have a word with Bernard Fox!'

Tolemy, Hodge, Bob Love and Drumnadrockit had adjourned to the portacabin office. The robot did not want his special relationship with Tolemy made known to the general public.

'Centuries ago,' explained Drumnadrockit, 'when the inhabitants of Vardon faced certain extinction, it was decided to preserve the memory of our race on a another planet.'

'As a robot?'

'That was our only option. But first we needed an ally on that planet. We needed someone who was wise, virtuous, unafraid. You, Tolemy, were created out of that need.'

Tolemy did not understand. 'But I wasn't born till hundreds of years after Vardon was destroyed.'

'You were already conceived in our imagination.'

Was that the reason, Tolemy wondered, for the extraordinary web of coincidence that surrounded him, the mesh of cosmic synchronicity that had shaped his destiny? He thought of all the strangers who had wandered so inexplicably into his life – from the late lamented Charlie

Protheroe to the Man in Black who had shared his dreams.

'Through psychotronic projection we structured your folk memory, creating an evolutionary nexus. Cause out of chaos, choice out of chance...'

'Why choose Earth?' interrupted Bob who was beginning to suspect the motives of this extinct alien race.

'Earth was strategically well placed. We were already in contact with its primitive inhabitants...'

'The prehistoric tribesmen who created Tolemy's Tomb!' cried Leslie Hastie who had wandered in, hoping to discuss his accounts with the boss.

'Not only the tribesmen of this island. Vardon treated with all the nations of your planet. Romans, Greeks, Egyptians...'

Tolemy remembered the ancient writing on the sarcophagus. Hodge, also, was thinking of the ancient civilisations of the Mediterranean who, for all their genius, could never have built a working robot.

Drumnadrockit seemed to read her mind. 'We had to allow time for Earth technology to reach a stage where it was capable of building a Vardon surrogate.'

Bob turned aggressively to the robot. 'So you people have been interfering with Earth since life here began?'

'We have never tampered with your *free will,*' said Drumnadrockit severely. 'We wish only to nurture on your planet the Vardon ideals of freedom, justice and humanity.'

'I seem to have heard that somewhere before,' observed Bob Love.

But no one was listening.

'Remarkable boy,' said Mr Fox, as he poured Henry Fraddon a dry sherry in his study at *Westaways*. 'Imaginative, resourceful. University material, no question about it.'

'I am particularly interested in his extra-curricular activities, Mr Fox. I understand he has certain interests in an old toy factory down by the canal?'

'Indeed?' Bernard Fox sipped his sherry and stared intently ahead at a picture of his old college hockey team. Mr Fox had noticed that he developed an excruciating migraine whenever he thought about Tolemy and his

Droop Street enterprise. He had no intention of encouraging an attack for the benefit of his visitor. 'I've had an idea,' said Mr Fox. 'My daughter has more experience with Tolemy on a social level. You ought to talk to her.'

A rather sullen Edwina was duly summoned to the study to be introduced to Henry Fraddon.

'Tell me about Tolemy,' said Mr Fraddon.

'Don't talk to me about Tolemy!' said Eddie Fox.

Justin Watkin, Henry Fraddon and General Spiby staggered down the aircraft steps onto the rainswept tarmac of RAF Tregolls. It had been an appallingly turbulent journey in the ministry's elderly Dove. Derek Bidmead, storm-wrapped in black oilskin and sou'wester, was waiting to welcome them. 'It always rains in Cornwall,' he announced gloomily as he led the visitors away to inspect the newly equipped workshops.

'Very impressive,' said the Minister blandly in his hospital-opening voice.

There was, however, amongst the gleaming, futuristic machinery no sign of actual manufacture. Technicians with double firsts from the best universities wandered aimlessly about the clinical suites, queued at the tiny canteen, made earnest phone calls on telephones with perspex hoods in the corridors. But nothing was being produced.

'I see no robots!' snarled the general who was in a curmudgeonly mood after their sick-making flight from Northolt.

The minister was also more than a little disappointed, for he had been looking forward to showing off the Department's new toys to his opposite number in Washington. 'When exactly can we expect to see an operational robot?'

Bidmead smiled obsequiously. 'As soon as you provide us with the rest of the data, Minister,' he replied, passing back the buck like a grenade with its pin removed.

General Spiby grew redder and redder. The veins on his neck and forehead throbbed like fire hoses. Some incomprehensible expletive burst from his lips. 'This is intolerable!' he exploded. 'There must be no delay!'

'Well, Fraddon?' said Justin Watkin as the general strode off in the highest dudgeon. 'What's to be done?'

'I'm working on it,' the civil servant assured him.

'We want results, not promises!' declared the minister in his electioneering voice.

'*Cherchez la femme*,' said Henry Fraddon.

'I beg your pardon?'

Fraddon explained how everyone in Turlow was covering up for the enigmatic Tolemy James. 'However, Minister, I have discovered a girl friend who may help us find the boy's operator. Edwina Fox.'

General Spiby stomped across the airfield, his whole body crepitating with fury. If he had stayed with the wingeing Minister and his lackey a moment longer he would surely have had some kind of breakdown. The general wondered if, perhaps, he was going mad.

He stumbled towards the perimeter fence beyond which the cliff edge gave way to the roaring Atlantic. He stared out into the swirling spray and rain, at one, in his rage, with the violence of the elements. Dimly visible, about half a mile down the coast, a high promontory pointed vaguely in the direction of North America. 'What is that?' Spiby asked a patrolling military policeman.

'That's Tintagel, sir,' said the MP, following the general's gaze. 'King Arthur's castle.'

What happened next must have lasted about thirty seconds from the point of view of the watching airman. For the general, it was the experience of a lifetime. Spiby tripped. The words *Tintagel* and *Arthur* triggered a massive implosion in his brain. His own identity spilled into an inner void. Some brooding spirit of the Universe which had been reaching out across the infinite darkness towards him now burst all shackles of time, race and space. It poured into the old soldier like matter into a black hole. With one hand he struggled to support himself against the wire, with the other he tried to shield his eyes from the blinding light.

'You all right, sir?' said the MP.

General Spiby slowly pulled himself together. He stood firm again and turned to the anxious airman. '*Sovan rux nibo koshagi Kosnak!'* he cried.

The autumn term had begun at Turlow Comprehensive. Tolemy and Eddie Fox sat in class together, refusing to speak to each other and avoiding one another's eyes.

By the time Tolemy arrived at Droop Street after his first day back at school the whole place had been transformed. Under the direction of Drumnadrockit the production line had been reorganised to build the new, improved robotic mechanism. Inside the sterile room was a large, transparent jar containing a faintly fizzing blue chemical. Wires ran from electrodes in the jar to a computer-controlled power source that Drumnadrockit had previously constructed from the Vardon components. On the submerged metal elements in the jar a metallic coral was slowly forming.

'What's this?' asked Tolemy.

'An intergrated processing system for the new cyber unit,' explained Drumnadrockit making a small adjustment to the console.

'You mean this is an artificial brain?'

'If you wish to think in anthropomorphic terms - yes,' said Drumnadrockit rather evasively, hurrying across to supervise another part of the assembly process.

One thing was now quite clear to Tolemy. The new, improved Drumnadrockit would be built in a fraction of the time it had taken to construct the original. The modified robot would be more sophisticated, more powerful - perhaps less subservient than the version they had put together themselves. The boy wondered if Bob Love was right and that they had started something that could never be stopped.

'No need to look so worried, Tolemy,' said Drumnadrockit reassuringly.

The feeling of panic subsided. All the same, Tolemy wished he could have talked things over with the professor.

But Professor Melmo rarely came to the factory these days. Since Drumnadrockit had been brought to life the scientist preferred to stay at the cottage enjoying the sunshine of an Indian summer in his chair under the apple tree. Sometimes Drumnadrockit (who complained of being bored left alone in the factory at night, but refused to have his power switched off) would arrange a lift in Leslie Hastie's car and come round for a chat. The two of them – like a couple of yokels yarning in the pub – would talk together until the small hours. The moths used to flutter around Drumnadrockit's bright eyes in the dark of the orchard while the robot told the scientist all he knew about Creation, Life and the Universe. Professor Melmo said very little during these nocturnal sessions, just nodded quietly and stroked Pythagoras who sat purring on his lap.

Eddie Fox arrived home from school to find a sleek, black Rover with uniformed chauffeur at the wheel under the monkey puzzle tree of *Westaways*. Her mother (whose services were not required that day at Citizens' Advice) was behaving as if half the Royal Family had stopped by for tea. She explained excitedly that two men from Whitehall were waiting in the sitting room. To see Edwina! (No one had told Mrs Fox of Henry Fraddon's earlier visit.)

Mrs Fox ushered Eddie into the sitting room and closed the door. She waited outside in the hall for a moment, hoping to catch a word or two, then hurried to the kitchen where a preserving pan of apple chutney was starting to catch.

Eddie recognised Mr Fraddon immediately.

'Good afternoon, Miss Fox. May I introduce General Spiby.'

The general, she observed, was older, bigger, more morose than Fraddon. His face hung in folds like a tree-fungus. He nodded, grunted, but made no effort – as yet – to shake her hand.

'My dear young lady,' Fraddon began. 'We have reason to believe that you can help us on a matter of national security.'

'Not Tolemy and his stupid robot again? Do me a favour!'

'We would like you to do *us* a favour.'

Eddie instantly regretted her words. Whatever temporary hostility she might feel toward Tolemy, she instinctively sided with her old friend against these pin-striped zombies.

Her outburst had, however, stirred the general into life. He began to jerk in his chair like the pneumatic model of the Michelin man in the window of the garage where Mrs Fox serviced her 2CV. He began to breathe heavily as if in the throes of a bad attack of asthma. He started to mutter but Eddie could not understand the blurred, guttural syllables. Eddie, hoping desperately that her mother would come back into the room with some tea or something, edged anxiously towards the door. The general leaned forward holding out a trembling hand. The skin was puckered and age-spotted, the fingers jaundiced with nicotine. Eddie stood rooted to the spot with disgust and embarrassment.

'Kosnak vor kawx minaro bor!' cried the general, tumbling forward out of his seat and onto one knee. *'Shashaa shashu?'* He clawed at the terrified girl.

Edwina felt a terrible energy pass between them. She sobbed and struggled for breath.

'Vizmanano kox Kosnak!' General Spiby grabbed her hand with his. There was a flash. The girl's body convulsed as if she were strapped in the electric chair. She screamed.

Mrs Fox rushed back into the sitting room to find her daughter unconscious on the floor.

Tolemy decided to have a factory party. It was a combined thank you to everybody for working so hard and a birthday celebration for Drumnadrockit. Drumnadrockit, of course, was about to have a second birthday. His new body – R2, as it was called until the intelligence transfer – was now complete. It rested in the sterile room, a bland, faceless, rather sinister figure – like a naked shop window dummy, waiting only for the matrix to be inserted. Tolemy much preferred the original hand-built robot to this anonymous new android, but Drumnadrockit couldn't wait to get rid of his old body.

Professor Melmo did not like parties but had been persuaded to come along so as to be present when the intelligence unit was inserted in R2. For the moment he stood aloof from the jollification, sipping a white wine and soda and talking to Drumnadrockit. 'What is so special about the new design?' he asked the robot curiously.

'A purely superficial enhancement,' said Drumnadrockit who had refused to explain the precise details of his modifications to any of the humans. 'Nevertheless, it is a performance factor which demands the ultimate of Vardon technology.'

'You look a bit down in the dumps,' said Tolemy, coming across to join the prof.

'To every action,' said Professor Melmo somberly, 'there is an equal and opposite reaction.'

'I remember,' said Tolemy.

'I have been giving the matter much thought,' said the scientist. 'I believe, my dear boy, that we have opened Pandora's Box!'

Doctor Poller had assured Mrs Fox that there was nothing seriously wrong with Eddie. 'Some sort of shock. A nervous trauma. Not uncommon in adolescent girls.' He recommended plenty of rest and promised to return the next day.

Eddie lay in bed staring up at the ceiling and refusing to speak to her mother or Bernard. Occasionally she would shiver and moan, sometimes talking excitedly to herself in an incomprehensible language. *'Zilosava min quinkkwa Kosnak!'*

'If she's not better by tomorrow evening, I'm getting a specialist,' said Mrs Fox to her husband. 'We can always claim it back on BUPA.'

That afternoon, while Mrs Fox was busy making Christmas puddings in the kitchen, Eddie, who had been asleep all morning, opened her eyes. She sat up, threw back the duvet, got out of bed and dressed herself. Moving as if in a trance, she descended the stairs, passed noiselessly through the hall and out through the front door.

No one saw Eddie Fox arrive at 68, Droop Street. She advanced down the deserted corridor towards the sterile room. The distant music and laughter sounded in her ears, but it was as remote as if it came from another planet. She entered the sterile assembly area.

Ignoring the draped figure that had been placed on the operating table, she moved straight to the cloning jar. R2's intelligence chip clung to the metal plate like a mollusc. Edwina Fox plunged her hands into the effervescence and ripped the spongy growth from its bed. The object in her hand began to steam and grow hot. As the energy flowed from the girl and into the cerebral core, Eddie's natural faculties returned and she felt the heat of the nodule like a hot cinder in her grasp. She rushed instinctively to the inhuman cadaver on the operating table. Her hand guided the intelligence unit to the vital orifice. Synthesised body met synthesised soul and the alien creature was whole.

Eddie, her mission accomplished, staggered dizzily to the corner of the room. She looked round, confused. Where the hell was she! She remembered cycling home from school . . . two men waiting for her in the sitting room. But she was not now in *Westaways*; it looked more to her like Tolemy's robot factory. But she had never seen this area before with its clinical fittings, surgical instruments, laboratorial tubes and tinctures . . .

Something was moving underneath the crumpled sheet on the table opposite. A hand emerged and pulled back the cover. The thing sat up.

'Tolemy!' cried Eddie in relief.

The boy, his lips bowed in a cruel, taut smile, swung his legs to the floor and stood unsteadily.

'What's going on?'

He made no reply but staggered towards the girl like a drunken stranger. He raised his hands as if to hug his old friend.

'Tolemy, no!' She could feel the tingle of static electricity jumping the gap between them and instinctively knew that the moment the boy's hand touched her she would be dead. She screamed.

Professor Melmo heard the cry as he tapped his way down the corridor. He was bored with the party and felt a strange desire to visit the assembly room – alone. He flung open the door.

Eddie Fox cowered in the corner, dominated by the creature that she had unwittingly brought to life on the operating table. The blind scientist could see none of this but sensed immediately that he was in the presence of great evil.

'What the devil!'

The creature turned towards the intruder. The professor lashed furiously about him with his stick. There was a sudden and excruciating whistling. It was the same ear-piercing screech that Eddie had heard that night with Tolemy on Turlow Heath. Like the treasure hunters on Tolemy's Tomb, the professor was now frozen in a cloud of dazzling luminence. His bones shone like an X-ray picture through his flesh and clothes. Eddie hid her head in her hands and curled up in a terrified ball on the floor.

Tolemy came running in followed by Hodge, Bob and Drumnadrockit. 'Eddie!' He ran straight to the trembling girl.

'Get away from me!' she screamed, recoiling from the boy. 'Tolemy tried to kill me,' she sobbed to Bob and Hodge.

'That's not possible,' protested Tolemy. 'I've only just come in.'

'That's right, love,' said Bob. 'We were all at the party.'

'Then what was that *thing*?' she stammered, relieved at least that Tolemy was still a normal creature of flesh and blood.

By now Hodge had spotted the empty table. 'Where's the robot?'

'Where's the professor?' said Tolemy anxiously.

'It was like that time on the heath.' Eddie tried to explain the awful phenomenon that had just recurred in the sterile room.

Drumnadrockit stood motionless, his psycho-sensors whirring frantically.

Tolemy ran across to a pile of clothes which he had spotted beside the door. He lifted up an old tweed jacket with leather patches on the elbows, a yellow bow tie and a broken white stick. 'Professor . . . No!' Tears welled in his eyes. Eddie knelt down beside the boy and put her arms around him. 'The professor saved my life,' she whispered.

'Something is very wrong,' announced Drumnadrockit.

Tolemy buried his head on Eddie's shoulder and wept.

That same afternoon a man entered the offices of the Turlow Building Society, pointed a gun (a Woolworth's toy, it later transpired) at a startled Gwyneth Powell and demanded that the entire cash float be handed over immediately. Miss Powell obediently passed across the best part of £35,000 in a mixture of new and used notes.

'Could you give me a description of the man?' said PC Barnfather whose patrol car had been the first to answer Kevin Kettle's 999.

'A description?' said Gwyneth Powell fortifying herself with a substantial creme de menthe from Kevin Kettle's cocktail cabinet. 'You don't need a description. I *know* him! We *all* do!'

'Is that a fact?' said Tom Rivers getting out his notebook.

'It was Leslie Hastie!'

When the police arrived at Tinkerbell Toys Mr Hastie assumed that it was to do with the unfortunate accident in the sterile room. He was surprised to find himself the centre of attention.

'Mr Hastie, we'd like you to come with us to the police station. In connection with our inquiries.'

'This is ridiculous!' retorted Bob Love as PC Barnfather explained the circumstances. 'Leslie's been in the factory all afternoon!'

'Mr Love is quite correct,' declared Drumnadrockit entering the office and joining in the conversation. 'Mr Hastie has an unbreakable alibi.'

Rivers and Barnfather stared at the silver apparition.

'This is Drumnadrockit,' said Tolemy. 'One of our range of special toys.'

The robot's eyes glittered.

'That thing's a *toy*?' stuttered Constable Barnfather.

'Anything else I can do to help, officer?' said Drumnadrockit, every inch the model citizen.

The two policemen, who had not been feeling themselves since the affair of the stolen Volvo, decided it was high time they returned to the police station.

'What the hell's going on?' demanded Bob Love as the two dumbfounded officers returned to their car.

'There has been an error,' declared Drumnadrockit.

'Eddie was attacked in the assembly room by someone she thought was *me*,' said Tolemy, white and shocked. 'Who then attacked and killed the professor.'

'After which a dead ringer for Leslie goes and holds up the TSB,' added Hodge.

'Something got into the host body. Something that can change the appearance of R2 at will.'

Bob Love turned accusingly to the robot. 'Just what is R2's special facility?'

'R2 was constructed inside a plasmic shield,' Drumnadrockit conceded grudgingly.

'Well, bugger me,' said Hodge, amazed rather than frightened by the alien technology. 'A disguise mechanism!'

'Would *you* want to look like *me*?' said Drumnadrockit pathetically. 'I wanted to be able to assume the outward appearance of a Vardon.'

'Or a *human being*!' retorted Bob Love angrily. All his worst fears were being realised.

'To every action,' said Tolemy to himself, 'there is an equal and opposite reaction.'

'Was I right? Or was I right!' said Bob.

'There is no need to worry,' Drumnadrockit assured them. 'The dissident entity will be tracked down and *deconstructed*!'

But no one else appeared to share the robot's confidence. 'R2 has turned into a killing machine,' said Tolemy, expressing all their fears. 'And a machine that can disguise itself as a human. We have created the ultimate transformer!'

CHAPTER SEVEN

Henry Fraddon had begun to doubt whether there would be any results from his investigation into Tinkerbell Toys. He had now interviewed teachers and parents, lawyers and land-agents, a deranged ex-manager of the Turlow Building Society and a curate with paint-stripping halitosis who ran the local youth club. No one could, or *would*, reveal the power behind the infuriating Tolemy James.

His final interview with Edwina Fox - far from being the break-through promised to the Minister - had been the most embarrassing disaster. (It had been a mistake to allow that old fool Spiby to accompany him to *Westways* - behaviour like that could land them both in the *News Of The World*.) Fraddon was on the verge of despair when he received an offer of help from a most unlikely source.

'Please come in, Mr Fraddon.' The civil servant was ushered, once more, into the tiny sitting room of the cottage on the edge of Turlow Heath. 'Do sit down!' Fraddon suddenly felt uneasy. There was something *different* about Professor Melmo.

'What will you have, Henry?'

'Oh, perhaps a small gin and tonic.' Fraddon watched his host as he moved to the cupboard in the corner. Something wasn't quite right... Of course! The man had abandoned his white stick.

Melmo poured a steady measure from the bottle of Gordon's and topped it up with tonic water. He handed the visitor his glass. 'Your good health.'

'You won't join me?'

'I don't drink any more.'

Fraddon sipped his gin, wondering what had happened to the obstinate old devil to have achieved both conversion and cure. 'I understand that you are now prepared to co-operate with the Ministry. Very wise, if I may say so.'

'How soon do we start?'

Fraddon was amazed at the man's enthusiasm. 'I suggest we fly down to Cornwall first thing in the morning.'

'Why not now? It is vital that we begin work without delay!'

Something pushed open the door of the sitting room and came in. 'Ah,' said Fraddon, feeling uncharacteristically well disposed to both man and beast. 'The famous Pythagoras.'

'Hello, puss,' said Melmo, half-heartedly attempting to stroke the ginger tom.

Pythagoras jumped backwards, hissing furiously.

Tolemy sat at the kitchen table in Beachcroft Close in front of a plate of congealed baked beans and sausage. Beside him was a copy of the local paper which he anxiously scanned for news of further mayhem in Turlow New Town.

'*Man Exposes Himself In Over-Sixties Bingo Session*. Could that be R2 on the rampage? I mustn't get paranoid!' Tolemy told himself sternly.

'You'll be late for school!' said Terry James coming in from the road where he was cleaning his lorry after a four day trip to Inverness.

'It's a Saturday.'

His dad began filling a fresh bucket of water at the sink. 'You'll be down the factory, then?' There was no answer from the boy. Mr James felt a sense of alienation. 'How are things in the doll business?'

Tolemy thought of the disastrous events at 68, Droop Street; how even now Bob and Leslie were taking it in turns to drive Drumnadrockit around the streets of Turlow in a desperate attempt to find R2 before the rogue robot could do any more damage. 'Oh, terrific!' he replied sourly.

The doorbell rang. Terry James peered out of the window, relieved not to have to continue the conversation.

'It's your girlfriend.' Wondering whether Edwina Fox could be responsible for the change in the lad, he took his bucket from the sink and moved to the back door. 'Hello, Eddie.'

'Morning, Mr James.' Eddie Fox closed the door behind Tolemy's father. 'Anything?' Tolemy shook his head. 'No news is good news.' She spotted the abandoned plate. 'At least have some breakfast. You've not eaten enough to keep a sparrow alive.'

Tolemy turned sharply towards Eddie, a guilty look on his face. 'Oh, no!'

'Now what?'

'Pythagoras!' said Tolemy, half an hour later, as they leaned their bicycles against the wall of Professor Melmo's cottage. 'He must be starving.' Tolemy felt for the key under the stone. He opened the front door and they went into the hall. Something warm and furry came from the shadows and rubbed itself, purring loudly, against Tolemy's legs.

'Doesn't seem very hungry to me,' said Eddie.

'Shh!' Someone was moving about in the kitchen. 'Hello?' said Tolemy nervously.

The kitchen door opened. 'Oh, it's you, Tol.'

'Mrs Erskine!' He'd forgotten about the professor's housekeeper. How on earth was he going to explain about the old boy's death.

'You've just missed his lordship, I'm afraid.'

'Who?'

'The prof. Who else?'

'Professor Melmo was here? *This morning*?'

'He does live here, you know.' Mrs Erskine had returned to the kitchen to resume work with a bowl of Flash.

'Did he say when he'd be back?' shouted Eddie from the hall.

As she rinsed the squeegee in the sink Mrs Erskine muttered something about his nibs going away to work for the government and the bother of coming in just to feed a cat. She put down the mop and returned to the door. 'Anything particular you wanted, Tol?'

But, by now, Tolemy and Eddie were away on their bikes, peddling furiously back into town.

*

Henry Fraddon did not really need to work on Saturday mornings, but he preferred pottering in the office to mowing the lawn at home or (perish the thought!) pushing a wire trolley for Mrs Fraddon in Wimbledon's Sainsburys. He was, therefore, at his desk, thinking vaguely about luncheon when the duty commissionaire phoned from reception. 'Two young persons to see you, sir,' Sergeant Major Grudge's parade ground voice echoed round the empty foyer. 'Miss Edwina Fox and Mr Tolemy James from Tinkerbell Toys.'

It had been Eddie's idea to go up to London and who had worked out the address of the Whitehall office from the directories in Turlow Public Library. 'R2 must be disguised as Professor Melmo,' she repeated to Tolemy as they rattled on the Circle Line between Paddington and Westminster. 'We've got to warn them!'

Fraddon smiled patronisingly at his young visitors. All was very right with the world. A remarkably co-operative Melmo was already at work with Bidmead in Cornwall, the Minister was off his back and those wretched Americans would soon have their noses put thoroughly out of joint by the dazzling expertise of their British rivals.

'It's about Professor Melmo,' Tolemy blurted out, still hot and flushed from their hurried journey.

'Ah, yes. Professor Melmo.' Henry Fraddon decided he *would* have that half bottle of Meursault '82 with his salmon at lunch, then, perhaps, an hour or two at Lords . . .

'Professor Melmo is dead.'

Fraddon laughed. 'I can assure you that the professor is very much alive.'

Tolemy caught his breath. Could they all have been wrong? Could Melmo really have survived? He felt Eddie's hand on his arm. There was no avoiding the awful truth. 'You *think* it's Melmo, but he's really a robot in disguise!'

The civil servant brayed with laughter.

'The real professor was killed by an android!' cried Eddie.

'In which case he has made a remarkable recovery.'

'Can I talk to him?' said Tolemy smartly.

'I'm afraid your friend has already left London,' replied Fraddon resuming his frigid smile.

'Where's he gone?'

Fraddon frowned as if the question was mildly indecent. But he was in a mood to humour the boy. 'Professor Melmo is, as you know, a leading expert in the field of servo-control systems, and he is currently working for Her Majesty's Government. Now, if you'll excuse me, I've an important appointment.'

'I'm sorry for being so beastly to you about your factory,' said Eddie as they snatched a quick hamburger in the Wimpy bar on Paddington Station.

Tolemy grinned. 'That's all right.' It was good having Eddie to rely on again.

'And I know how you must be feeling about the professor.'

Tolemy nodded. 'I think he knew he was going to die. He'd sort of come to the end of the road.'

'Don't worry, Tolemy. It'll be all right. You see.'

'It had better be!' said Tolemy, grabbing the last of the chips.

Drumnadrockit's interpretation of the data was not reassuring. 'If R2 is working for the Government, he will be able to build a robot of equal sophistication to himself.'

'And as treacherous?' Eddie well remembered the attack she witnessed in the sterile room.

'That is the logical conclusion.'

Hodge, Tolemy, Bob and Eddie were all silent, each thinking of the appalling danger. A malevolent robot was at large: cunning, undetectable and capable of replicating itself.

'But how did R2 get itself programmed with an ideology that is entirely alien to Vardon *and* Earth?' said Hodge.

Drumnadrockit remained as mute as if his power supply had been switched off. Tolemy now knew how to interpret the robot's moods. The anthropoid had information he did not wish to be accessed by the humans. Hodge's remark reminded the boy of a curious and disturbing name that the Professor and General Spiby had both summoned as if from the air itself. 'Tell me,' said Tolemy turning to Drumnadrockit. 'Who are the Kosnaks?'

There was a sudden fierce buzzing from the robot. His eyes flashed. 'Kosnaks do not exist!' he declaimed.

'Then how did Melmo and Spiby get to know...'

'All Kosnaks were destroyed.'

'How?' said Bob.

'Where?' cried Hodge.

'When?' cried Tolemy.

'In the war with the Vardons,' the robot informed them. 'The entire Vardon race was eliminated. So too was that of the Kosnaks.'

'Mutually Assured Destruction,' muttered Bob Love grimly. 'You're just the sort of friend we need on Earth, I don't think!'

Eddie began to whimper like a tormented animal.

'There is evil!' warned Drumnadrockit.

Eddie screamed. *'Vishmaneo Kosnak!'*

Hodge grabbed her by the shoulders, shook her roughly and slapped her face. Eddie blinked. 'What happened?' she whispered in a distressed but normal voice.

'Some kind of *possession* if you ask me,' said Bob.

Tolemy now had a good idea of what kind of evil spirit had invaded his friend. If the racial memory of the Vardons had been perpetuated beyond their physical demise, why not that of their arch-enemies the Kosnaks? 'Could something have passed from the General into the matrix of R2?' he asked the robot.

'It is *possible*,' said Drumnadrockit slowly.

'Transmitted through me?' Eddie thought back to her traumatic encounter with the old soldier at *Westaways*.

'It is *probable*,' Drumnadrockit up-dated alarmingly.

'So, just as you're a representative of Vardon,' interrupted Bob, 'R2 is now a *Kosnak* supporter?'

Drumnadrockit agreed. Yet another resurrection had taken place on Earth.

'You'd better tell us what these Kosnaks are all about!'

'Domination, control, power, territorial ambition...' Drumnadrockit's description was not very reassuring for the frightened humans.

'So what it boils down to is this,' said Tolemy. 'R2, with the help of the British Government, is now constructing a bunch of Kosnak robots?'

'Affirmative,' said Drumnadrockit.

'A new race of Kosnaks who could destroy the world as we know it!'

'With regret, yes,' announced the Vardon robot.

'But we can't let that happen!' shouted Tolemy. 'We must *do* something!'

'I agree,' said Drumnadrockit.

'Just as well, since it's all *your* fault in the first place,' added Bob Love grumpily. 'I suppose this is the great evil you wanted to protect us from. An evil created by *you*!'

Drumnadrockit refused to get drawn into an argument. 'The Kosnaks must be destroyed!' he declared simply.

'Any bright ideas how you strip down a mechanical alien with a pocketful of deadly weapons?'

Drumnadrockit had only one answer: 'We *too* must build more robots!'

With a shriek from the tyres and a roar of the braking engines the State Department jet put down on Tregolls main runway.

'This Siberia?' said Charity O'Toole as she peered out at the cold, grey drizzle.

'Sorry,' said Henry Fraddon from under a large black umbrella at the bottom of the steps. 'It always rains in Cornwall.' He guided the American and her two military colleagues towards the waiting car.

'Where the heck are you taking us, Henry?' said Charity O'Toole as the car sped past the laboratory buildings, past the guard house and away from the base.

'A sentimental whim of General Spiby.' The British civil servant smiled archly. 'But I promise you the demonstration will be worth our little detour.'

Ms O'Toole was less than enthralled with their Cornish mystery tour. 'Just so long as there's no live bullets!' she snapped.

They descended into the village with its prim granite villas, abandoned ice cream kiosks and boarded-up souvenir emporia. Then out past the breeze-block retirement bungalows, along the coast, and into a wild cove where they stopped in a small car park already full of other official-looking vehicles.

'Siberia-on-Sea?' inquired Charity O'Toole as her stiletto heels sank up to the hilt in the cold wet sand.

'Tintagel,' Fraddon replied a trifle haughtily.

'Isn't that the name of a movie or something?' said the man from the US Army.

'King Arthur's castle, actually.' The civil servant pointed up at the rocky promontory above them.

'Where's the helicopter?' said the man from the US Airforce.

'We walk.' Fraddon indicated a flight of stone steps that wound up the cliff.

'Henry, you jest!' protested Ms O'Toole. But the Englishman was already climbing to the ruined battlements.

Up on the high plateau the wind and spray from the sea scoured the ruined walls of the twelfth-century castle. Technicians and observers huddled in the relative shelter of the old keep while General Spiby, in full dress uniform, strode about the crumbling ramparts impatiently waiting for the spectators to assemble.

Henry Fraddon arrived at the top of the cliff path with his breathless and bedraggled American contingent to be greeted by the Right Honourable Justin Watkin. Fraddon signalled to the parapet that the VIPs were ready whereupon Spiby descended the steps like the hero of an operatic melodrama. Without saying a word, the general led the way to an open courtyard on the west side of the keep where a statuesque figure stood shrouded beneath a black tarpaulin. The spectators, mindful of the events of Turlow Heath, kept a respectful distance.

'Ladies and gentlemen,' Spiby's voice ricocheted around the jagged walls. 'Welcome to the fabled birthplace of Arthur Pendragon. Today we bring to life another great warrior.' He abruptly tore the tarpaulin from the object beneath.

The spectators peered curiously at the general's latest panjandrum. It seemed to be neither man nor machine, rather a human-sized, bi-pedal insect. The synthetic matter of its torso (a green mixture – half metal, half plastic) appeared not to have been *constructed* but *grown*, like a fungus. Tubes and tendrils hung about its hard, ribbed body like the gnarled roots of a tree. It had the head of an overblown cockroach with sharp horns and a cruel mouth. It was altogether monstrous.

General Spiby stood proudly beside the cyber-creature. He nodded curtly towards one side of the courtyard. Someone stepped forward from the group of technicians and walked towards the new robot.

'That's Professor Melmo,' explained the Minister to Ms O'Toole. 'The professor has masterminded all our latest developments.'

The architect of the new robot inserted a small cartridge behind the beast's head. There was a faint buzzing. The creature's deceitful, crocodile eyes flickered.

'Arise, Sir Galahad!' cried General Spiby excitedly (if somewhat inappropriately).

'To rise I first must kneel,' intoned the robot in a hard cruel voice. He quivered, and turned to the general. 'A Kosnak kneels before no man!'

The spectators moved closer, curious to hear the machine's conversation.

'Sir Galahad, arise!' repeated the general nervously.

'My name is not Galahad, but Modred!' the cyber-warrior continued.

General Spiby stared back at his new creation, confused and dismayed.

'Mildred?' said Justin Watkin. 'I don't call that a very suitable name for a war machine.'

'Modred, Minister,' Fraddon corrected him. 'Another Knight of the Round Table.'

'You will observe,' said Melmo, taking over the demonstration, 'that our new prototype is fully mobile and articulate.'

Modred, as he had called himself, stepped forward and walked amongst the amazed visitors like an uninvited and potentially violent guest at a cocktail party. 'Better than the last contraption,' Charity remarked to her Army colleague. 'But he's not what I call *attractive*.'

'I am designed to be functional, indomitable, not beautiful!' declaimed the robot, whose hearing was nothing if not acute.

'You will observe the prototype's ballistic capabilities,'

Melmo announced.

Modred raised an arm towards a rock about three feet from the American delegation. There was a flash, a dull thud and the rock burst into fragments.

'Oh, boy!' exclaimed the USAF Major, stepping sharply backwards with the rest of the VIPs.

'I say, well done, Melmo,' murmured the delighted Minister.

The hideous cyber-beetle turned and marched to the cliff edge. It raised a hand towards the sea where a raft floated about half a mile off shore. There was another flash and the raft disappeared leaving only a cloud of steam above the rolling Atlantic.

The audience applauded enthusiastically. The American army officer was beside himself with excitement. 'If we could send a few of those into Iran, Nicaragua...'

'I'm impressed,' said Charity O'Toole to the Minister.

Justin Watkin grinned like a schoolboy. 'You ain't seen nothing, yet!'

'Any chance we could arrange another demo? Maybe when the President comes over for the London summit?'

'Congratulations, Arthur.' Henry Fraddon clapped General Spiby on the back. 'I always said robots were the infantry of the future.'

The general grunted. 'Why does the damn thing want to call itself Modred!'

'A Knight by any other name.' The civil servant gazed across at the unlovely creature prowling on the cliff edge. 'Maybe not in shining armour, but...'

'Modred betrayed King Arthur,' replied the general. 'His name is a byword for treachery and deceit!'

Drumnadrockit returned to the secret Vardon hoard to collect more alien materials and components for his companion robots. This time, however, Tolemy forbade the anthropoid even to *think* of borrowing Mr Fox's car. Instead, Bob Love hired a large van which they parked alongside the ploughed field where the two policemen had had their first encounter with the Vardon surrogate. But only Tolemy was allowed to follow Drumnadrockit into the secret chamber in the rock which opened up at the coded signal transmitted by the robot. Tolemy gazed, stupefied, at the Aladdin's cave. 'Are there places like this elsewhere on Earth?'

'Of course. Your planet was an important staging point in Vardon's trade with the rest of the Galaxy.'

Tolemy thought about all the energy points on Leslie Hastie's maps. 'Did Earth people never break in?'

'There is a powerful auto-protect system.'

Tolemy agreed, and shivered as he remembered poor Roy Smart and Jimmy Monk on Turlow Heath. 'But what about R2?'

'His matrix is automatically programmed with the Vardon passcode.'

'So he can build more Kosnak robots from Vardon components?'

'Affirmative,' said Drumnadrockit. 'Which is why there is no time to be lost!'

First of the new robots off the Droop Street production line was a scaled-down replica of Drumnadrockit himself. He was short and paunchy with a coal scuttle hat. Drumnadrockit insisted that they all wait until Tolemy came round after school before inserting the final vital component.

A cartridge containing the cloned matrix was inserted in a slot at the back of the Mark 2 robot's neck. There was a click, a metal cough and a frenzied whirring.

'Something wrong?' queried Tolemy.

'Not at all,' said Drumnadrockit. 'Verbal data is being scanned. A process of self-nomenclature is part of the boot-up.'

'It's choosing a name for itself!' said Hodge, laughing.

The whirring abruptly stopped. 'Hello, everybody,' said the new robot. 'My name is Osmoses.'

'Bit of a mouthful,' said Tolemy.

'You can call me Os,' suggested Osmoses. 'Or Moses if you prefer.'

'Hi, Os,' said Hodge.

Next to be engendered was an amazing piece of work which bore no resemblance to a human being whatsoever. Its body consisted of a sphere some two feet in diameter to which was attached eight jointed tentacles. This weird and wonderful contraption was crowned with a single eye like a belisha beacon. Tolemy decided it was an octopus.

'More like a vacuum cleaner, if you ask me,' said Bob.

'I am Number Three,' said the mechanism modestly after a moment's reflection.

'That's not very imaginative,' said Tolemy.

'I am designed for physical dexterity not abstract thought,' said Number Three indignantly. To demonstrate his mobility he careered around the room like an excited top then ran up the wall, across the ceiling and down the other side.

Bob Love stood with his hand in his pockets looking very disapproving. There was a round of applause from the rest of the humans.

'Please don't encourage him to show off!' groaned Osmoses.

The fourth member of the metal family was a different kettle of fish altogether. Its body was a cylinder supported, parallel with the ground, on four short legs. For sensors it had a tail at the rear while at the front there were whiskers and pointed ears on its small round head. Drumnadrockit had obviously been observing Pythagoras on his visits to the professor's cottage.

'Miaow...' said the little auto-beast.

'Hello, puss!' said Tolemy, absolutely entranced.

'My name is Mog,' the creature corrected him.

'Why a *cat*?' said Hodge.

'Everybody needs a cat!' said Drumnadrockit.

'And I am the very cat's whiskers of a cat,' added Mog. 'I listen, I watch, I wait. I go in secret places.' With a purring noise his little ears revolved like radar antennae (which is exactly what they were).

For the next robot in the team, Drumnadrockit reverted to an anthropoid shape. But there were some startling differences between the newcomer and Drumnadrockit or Osmoses. 'He reminds me of someone,' said Bob Love, peering at the inanimate body.

'Well, for a start, it's a *she* not a *he*!' retorted Hodge.

'I see. The token female?'

'Chauvinist pig!'

'A pig?' protested Osmoses. 'We're having no more

pseudo-animals!'

Mog gently hissed as Bob Love gazed down at the sleeping figure on the production line. The sensing units in the new model's scalp were shaped into a brillo pad of curly hair. A coy lurex bow was tied round the neck. The accessories which Drumnadrockit and Osmoses carried round the waist were contained in a metal reticule on the robot's arm. Her silver oversuit followed her female contours like the breastplate of a Valkyrie. 'Oh, my God! It's the Iron Lady!' cried Bob Love, who was not exactly an admirer of Britain's first woman Prime Minister.

'I think Drumnadrockit's been watching too much TV,' said Hodge, handing over another matrix.

The Senior Robot placed the intelligence unit inside the last android's silver handbag. The warrior maiden opened her eyes and sat up.

'Hello, Tin Lizzy,' said Hodge.

'My name is Marcia,' announced the female of the species. 'No smoking!' A thin, sharp finger stabbed at the empty pipe in Bob Love's mouth.

The lady robot looked around the assembly room with the air of a dowager accustomed to more seemly accommodation. 'Goodness me,' she declared in a ringing, schoolmarm's voice. 'This place is so untidy!'

It was raining, as usual, at closing time in the Cornish village of Gwenarthy when Joe Pengelly left the Miners Arms and set off for his lonely cottage on the cliff. He turned up the collar of his old army greatcoat as he took the rough track that led along the coast and past the abandoned mines. It was a dark and treacherous route, but Joe knew it like the back of his hand – even with several pints of best St Austell Ale inside him.

As he passed the ruined engine house of Wheal Tregolls, Joe (who was a staunch Methodist) began to sing to himself, 'Oh God our help in ages past . . .' The going was easier now and there was some illumination from the security lights of the nearby base.

Something moved behind the derelict winding house a few yards to his right. A rabbit, perhaps, or a dog? A stone was disloged – too heavy for an animal. 'Who's there?'

shouted Joe. There was the sound of dragging feet. 'What you be up to, then?' Something appeared from behind the ruined wall. Joe gasped. It was a nightmare creature with the feet of a man and the body and head of an insect. The beast had sharp antennae which whined like a telegraph wire and venomous eyes that gleamed at the terrified Cornishman.

Joe turned to run, but out of the darkness behind him another monstrous form stepped forward. And a third, and then a fourth. Joe bent down to pick up a stone, but, before he could even stand upright again, he was paralysed by a terrible howl from the apparitions which surrounded him. Then everything was annihilated by searing white light.

CHAPTER EIGHT

Charity O'Toole smiled across at the Minister like a toothpaste advertisement. 'We have reserved twenty minutes in the President's schedule following next Sunday's summit talks at Lancaster House.'

Justin Watkin nodded. 'I'm sure that will be ample time to persuade the President of the efficacy of our anthropoid technology.'

Ms O'Toole agreed. Her Tintagel report had created a sensation in the Pentagon.

Henry Fraddon placed a folder on the desk between them. 'I have arranged with Professor Melmo for the display to take place on Horseguards' Parade.

'I say, what a splendid idea!' The Minister warmed with enthusiasm.

'The Mall and St James Park will, of course be closed.'

'Like a military tattoo,' continued Justin Watkin. 'A programme of thrills and spills. Perhaps a regimental band?'

'Leave it to me, Minister,' said the civil servant. 'I'm sure the new robots from Tregolls will be spectacular!'

General Spiby was working on the final details of his Grand Robotic Tournament when Inspector Cordingly came to see him in the Annex (which grew colder and damper as winter took its course).

'I need permission for my people to visit RAF Tregolls,' Cordingly explained.

'Out of the question, Charles,' barked the general. 'A load of local bobbies poking their noses in. That's the last thing we want.' But the general owed Cordingly a few favours. 'What exactly is the problem?' he added in a more reasonable tone. 'Maybe I can sort something out with RAF security.'

Inspector Cordingly took some papers from his dispatch case. 'Six people have now disappeared from the village next to RAF Tregolls. In each case a bundle of the missing person's clothing was discovered somewhere on the cliffs.'

Spiby heard inside his head a voice that he had desperately been trying to forget. '*I am Modred*!' He cast his own doubts resolutely aside. There was no turning back now. 'So?' he snapped. 'We're not the Salvation Army.'

'The Gwenarthy disappearances bear a remarkable similarity to the Monk-Smart business on Turlow Heath.'

The general began to shake his head violently, reluctant to hear more evidence.

But the inspector was determined to be heard. 'If your robots are half as smart as the creatures at Tinkerbell Toys...'

'For God's sake, Charles!' the general interrupted him angrily. 'Where's your sense of patriotism? We're on the brink of a major revolution in the way we police this country and you're worrying about a few Cornish yokels...'

'Human lives, General!' Cordingly began to wonder if Arthur Spiby had finally taken leave of his senses. 'I believe your robots are killing human beings!'

Spiby scowled. 'I refuse to consider the question.' His hands were trembling. 'I'm going to see Great Britain walk tall again. And no jumped-up thief-catcher is going to stop me!'

68, Droop Street had been turned virtually overnight into a munitions factory. A vast arsenal of weapons had now been assembled - laser blasters, program scramblers, body mines - all dedicated to destroying enemy robots. Some of these devices were integrated in the functions of Drumnadrockit, Marcia, Osmoses, Mog and Three. Others were self contained units to be used by their human allies.

Bob Love viewed the whole process with grim disapproval. He could see the world becoming a battleground for these manifestations from space who were continuing, on his own planet, a war that both sides had already lost. He cursed himself for having helped build Drumnadrockit.

Tolemy did his best to reassure his friend, trying at the same time to finish the homework he was doing for Mr Fox.

'Bash them! Bash them!' howled Os, bouncing up and down like a prize fighter as Three, his eight arms waving in all directions, completed the assembly of the hundredth armour blaster.

'Calm down, Osmoses,' said Marcia in her superior voice as she examined the circuit of a vapouriser unit.

'Shut your face, Tin Lizzy!' rasped Os.

'My name is Marcia,' the regal robot reprimanded him.

Bob Love looked round at all the armaments. He shook his head. 'It's not even as if we know where the Kosnak robots are hiding.'

Mog's little ears twitched. 'We have a visitor,' the cat robot warned.

'Inspector Cordingly,' announced Drumnadrockit, ever the perfect Jeeves, as he led the man from Scotland Yard into the factory.

'I'll get rid of him, Tol. No sweat,' said Osmoses stepping aggressively forward.

'He comes as a friend,' interposed Mog.

'Now then, officer,' said Marcia primly. 'What can we do to help?'

Inspector Cordingly surveyed the Ferrous Five with as much equanimity as he could manage. 'These are all your robots?' he stammered, wondering just who the female anthropoid reminded him of.

'That's right, Inspector,' said Tolemy.

Charles Cordingly's blood ran cold. Last time he visited the factory (albeit illegally) there was only one of them. If Spiby's creatures down in Cornwall were half as intelligent as this little mob and could replicate with the same speed the whole world was in the most terrible danger. 'Mr James,' he declared gravely. 'I need your help.'

General Spiby undid his seatbelt as the RAF Andover came to rest beside a couple of Nimrod patrol planes on the apron of the Cornish base. It had been a swift but spartan flight from London's Northolt airfield – rather like travelling in an empty Pickford's van as all but the front two rows of seats of the airliner had been removed to make room for the robots which were due on parade next day in Whitehall.

'There's no steps!' said the flight orderly as he opened the aircraft door.

The general grunted disapprovingly. What did these people think they were playing at? He had already made several phone calls to Tregolls to discuss arrangements for the Presidential demonstration but had been unable to speak to Melmo or Bidmead – or even the merest technician.

'Hang on, General,' said the orderly. 'I'll just winch down the on-board stairs.'

'Lucky the cloud base was high,' said Flight-Lieutenant Glaister joining them from the cockpit. 'I had to make a visual approach. Air traffic control seems to have gone on leave!'

Spiby peered out into the darkness. The security lights reflected coldly from the wet tarmac. He could hear the distant cry of gulls wheeling round the cliffs. But there was no sign of human life anywhere on the airfield.

'This is a queer show,' muttered Glaister as he led the way down the narrow metal ladder.

They walked together along the asphalt path towards the administration block and the construction labs. It was as if they had come to a ghost town.

'Reminds me of the bush,' said the orderly. 'With all the animals watching and waiting out of sight.' He laughed nervously.

Lieutenant Glaister stumbled over something on the path. He picked up a blue tunic and trousers. 'Somebody's uniform!'

'No discipline in this place,' growled the general (who had always regarded the RAF as a second class service).

'There's someone between those two huts,' whispered the aircraftman.

'Advance and be recognised!' ordered the general.

Slowly, something huge and heavy lumbered forward

from the shadows.

'Bloody hell!' gasped Glaister as he caught sight of the hideous cyber-insect.

A whirring sound came from the alien machine. It echoed around them like cicadas in a tropical night as other horrid clones moved forward from their hiding places. They were surrounded.

'It's all right,' said the general. 'These are our robots.'

'You mean those things are supposed to be on our side?' said the orderly, unconvinced.

'Think of them as intelligent tanks,' said the general.

The machines trundled ominously forward. 'You *sure* they're friendly?' whispered Flight-Lieutenant Glaister.

The general remembered again the evil voice at Tintagel. '*I am Modred.*'

'Good evening, General.' Spiby spun round. Professor Melmo had appeared, as if from nowhere, and stood beside him on the path.

'Ah, Melmo. What the devil's going on?'

'Where's the Commanding Officer?' demanded Glaister.

Melmo ignored both questions. 'Gentlemen, you will please continue to the parade ground.'

Derek Bidmead was waiting for them with a group of senior technicians as they passed the admin block. The escorting robots began to buzz like angry wasps as they sensed the presence of the civilians.

'Kosnaks will be supreme, Vardons will be destroyed,' Bidmead and his colleagues chanted as one, raising their hand in a Nazi-style salute.

Glaister stared at them in disgusted amazement. 'What was all that about?'

'Control code. For the robots,' muttered Bidmead uncomfortably.

The scientists fell in with the military and the escorting machines. Bidmead worked his way into a position where he was beside the general and as far as possible from any of the marching cyber-insects. 'We've had a few problems,' he whispered. 'The robots have become very – demanding.'

'Silence!' shrieked a metal monster.

'Sorry,' grovelled Bidmead.

'*Sorry*?' protested the Flight-Lieutenant, shocked to see a grown man apologise to a machine.

'Humans will not speak!' screamed another robot.

'What's been the trouble, then?' said the general to Melmo.

'No trouble, General. Everything is going according to plan. We are all now prepared to leave for London – where I look forward to meeting the President of the United States.'

They passed a line of huts and turned into a small tarmac parade ground, floodlit as if for a football match. For a moment Lieutenant Glaister imagined they had discovered the missing airforce personnel in the vast platoon that occupied the square. He realised, as they grew closer, that the company on parade consisted, not of men, but more vile automata.

Melmo raised his right arm. 'Kosnaks supreme! Vardons destroyed!' he cried.

'Kosnaks supreme! Vardons destroyed!' chorused the harsh, metallic voices of a hundred robots.

Melmo turned to Arthur Spiby. 'Is our work not well done, Earthling General?'

Spiby was overwhelmed. It was more than he had ever dreamed of. And yet . . .

'Power! Domination! Control!' chanted Melmo.

'Power! Domination! Control!' screamed the robots in reply.

'Let us begin the Great Task,' said the robot leader to the General. 'We shall subjugate this island. We shall put all nations of Earth under the Kosnak yoke. We shall rule the world!'

'Kosnaks shall rule the world!' roared the robots like the crowd at a Cup Final.

'*I am Modred*,' said a small voice in Spiby's head. Too late, the old soldier realised the prophetic truth of the first robot's words.

'Prepare for embarkation,' ordered Melmo, whereupon the surrogate Kosnaks began to march off the parade ground in the direction of the waiting aeroplane.

'Now, just you listen to me,' said Flight-Lieutenant Glaister to the man he supposed to be Professor Melmo. 'If you think I'm having anything more to do with this mad, fascist scheme...'

'Get down!' yelled Bidmead.

A ball of blue phosphorescence flew from one of the robot guards who remained with the party. Glaister instantly hit the deck and the enemy bolt passed over his head, impacting, some hundred yards behind him, with the Officers' Mess which collapsed in a pile of rubble.

'Don't you understand?' screamed the Head of Research hysterically. 'The machines have taken over! They're...' A white ray darted from another robot. Bidmead was silent. His empty clothes deflated onto the ground. The surviving humans froze.

'Well, gentlemen,' said Melmo. 'It's up to you. Co-operate or die!'

The humans were speechless. They were also watching with horror a whirling ball that came bowling towards them from the perimeter fence. Another fiendish device, no doubt, from the robot production line. The new mechanism stopped a few feet behind Melmo and the robot guards. Stationary, it looked to the terrified men like a giant spider. The cyber-Kosnaks whirred, sensing a presence. As they turned the new arrival held up a small box in one of its eight arms. There was a high pitched tone. The robots began to crackle like static on a radio. The insect creatures wobbled and swayed, while a quivering Melmo groaned.

'Take cover!' announced the octopoid.

The humans wasted no time in rushing to the shelter of one of the nearby workshops.

'Fire!' cried the octopoid in a high, tin voice.

From three points in the surrounding darkness, balls of energy and beams of super-laser power rushed at the stunned Kosnaks who each burst apart like a ruptured fuel tank, merging together in a huge balloon of fire.

Inspector Cordingly had phoned the Head of Special Branch direct from Tinkerbell Toys. 'We must destroy the enemy robots at once, sir,' he explained. 'They are agents of a hostile alien race.' After a small pause, the Commander – who was fully occupied protecting the visiting Heads of Government – suggested that the inspector had been overworking and should take some leave. Cordingly banged down the phone in despair. 'No one will believe me!'

'Closed minds,' muttered Leslie Hastie bitterly. 'I know just how you feel.'

'It's up to us then,' said Tolemy. 'The inspector knows where the Kosnaks are and *we* have the power to fight them!'

They set off within the hour, leaving Hodge and Eddie in charge of the office at Tinkerbell Toys. Bob, Leslie and the inspector took it in turns to drive the rent-a-van while Tolemy travelled in the back with the Vardon robots and a crate of anti-android weapons.

'Here we go, here we go, here we go!' hollowed Osmoses as they raced down the M4.

'Do be quiet, Osmoses!' said Marcia in her schoolmistress's voice.

'Belt up, yourself, Tin Lizzy,' retorted Os.

It was growing dark as the van crossed the Tamar bridge into Cornwall and turned right towards the north coast. They parked in a picnic spot on the cliffs a mile outside Gwenarthy and proceeded through the gorse towards the outer limits of Tregolls Air Base.

Mog gave a sudden squeak of alarm. 'Metal object approaching at one thousand feet!'

'Hide!' shouted Tolemy as a plane droned in over the sea on its final approach.

'Visitors?' said Bob from inside the cover of a large clump of bracken.

Leslie Hastie crawled out of a blackberry bush and dusted down his blazer and trousers. 'That was a transport aircraft. Looks like they're planning to ship something *out*.'

'They're taking the robots to London,' said Inspector Cordingly.

'London is full of the world's leaders,' whispered Bob Love.

'Precisely,' observed the inspector.

'All clear,' said Mog, his ears flapping.

'Forward!' cried Drumnadrockit.

The Ferrous Five and their three human allies arrived at the wire opposite the far end of the runway. Mog did another quick twirl of his super-sensitive ears. 'Many Kosnaks!' He pointed towards some buildings beyond the runway.

Tolemy was peering through the mesh at the Andover parked about a hundred yards in front of them. 'We mustn't let the Kosnak robots escape from here!'

'Cut the wire. We're going in,' said Inspector Cordingly.

'No!' Mr Hastie, with his two years' national service behind him, was something of an expert on fences. 'It'll only set off an alarm in the guard room.'

'Destroy the guardroom!' growled Os.

'Leave it to me,' said Three. He scurried up the barricade like a fly up a wall. Perched on top of the fence he extended one of his eight arms like the jib of a crane, lifting Tolemy clear of the wire and depositing him safe on the other side. In similar fashion the two remaining humans and the other metal creatures were helped over the barrier.

'Perhaps we can put the plane out of action?' suggested Tolemy.

'Good idea,' said Inspector Cordingly who wanted the boy away from the shooting. 'You go with Her Ladyship while the rest of us attack the main group of Kosnaks.'

'*My name is Marcia*!' protested the female robot.

Tolemy and the Iron Lady approached the Andover, hidden from the main building by several large crates which stood on the apron waiting to be loaded on to the plane. The boy's attention was immediately drawn to a long, coffin-like box resting by its own on the tarmac. He lifted the hinged lid and gasped at the sight which met his eyes.

'A human shape,' said Marcia, peering over the boy's shoulder at the contents of the box.

Tolemy gazed at the lifeless body. 'That,' he stammered, 'is the President of the USA!'

'It is a robot,' said the metal lady. 'Though not yet activated.'

'Another super-transformer? Like Professor Melmo? We must destroy him at once!' he cried.

But it was too late. An army of Kosnaks was already

advancing across the tarmac, ready to board the plane. 'They're *horrible*!' he gasped.

Marcia took what looked like a red billiard ball from her pack of light weapons.

'No!' hissed Tolemy. It was obvious that if they did anything to draw the Kosnaks' fire they would be hopelessly outnumbered.

Marcia reluctantly returned the grenade to her handbag.

Tolemy looked anxiously down at the imitation president. He thought of the chaos that would ensue if the Kosnaks ever left Tregolls with this extraordinary automaton. He had an idea. 'Have you got a program scrambler in that bag of yours?'

'These days,' said the Ferrous Female taking a small silver box from her reticule, 'a lady should be prepared for any eventuality.'

Tolemy removed the scrambler from the robot's grasp. The intricate mechanism inside the unit had been specially designed by Drumnadrockit to radiate a high frequency interference pattern which would paralyse the neuro-systems of the cyber-insects.

'There are too many of them!' warned Marcia as the army of Kosnaks marched inexorably towards them. 'The scrambler has only a limited range.'

'I know,' said Tolemy, slipping the silver box into the jacket pocket of the dummy president.

'I don't understand.'

'Lateral thinking!' The boy grinned and slipped his fingers into the robot's handbag, feeling for the matrix which had been inserted back in the Droop Street laboratory.

'Tolemy, what are you doing!'

'Sorry, Tin Lizzy.'

'My name is M...'

The Iron Lady lapsed into silence.

'There's hundreds of them!' exclaimed Bob Love as they watched the Kosnaks leave the square on their way to the waiting aircraft.

'If we attack now, they will destroy us,' observed

Drumnadrockit dispassionately.

'Well, bugger me!' said Os who had been looking forward to a good scrap.

'Language, Osmoses,' muttered Leslie Hastie. (He would have to insist that Hodge stopped swearing in front of the impressionable android).

'Look!' Bob had spotted the robotic shape of Professor Melmo. He could hardly believe that it was not the old boy himself.

The inspector was more concerned with the humans – three civilians and three servicemen, surrounded by four aggressive Kosnak guards. There seemed to be some sort of argument... Suddenly all hell was let loose. Within seconds the building to the right of them was razed to the ground in a burst of blue fire, while, in front of them, one of the hostages was atomised. (Alas, poor Bidmead.)

'Get in there with a program scrambler!' Drumnadrockit ordered Three. 'Osmoses and Leslie take the left flank. Inspector, you and Bob come with me to the right. When the humans are clear, open fire!'

They dashed heroically forward clutching a small silver box. The radiation from the device engulfed the Kosnak guards and the cyber Melmo, jamming their control systems. Each vile creature succumed instantly (if only temporarily) to helpless paraplegia. The humans lost no time in making good their escape, whereupon Osmoses – with deadly accuracy – hurled a magnetic grenade at the bogus professor which knocked the super-transformer smouldering to the ground.

Beside Os, Leslie Hastie blazed away with his newly acquired bazooka. Bob Love, from the cover of the NAFFI extension, took from the inspector a small, heavy grey ball which he rolled in the direction of the disintegrating automata.

A few feet from the works manager, Drumandrockit, activating a circuit on his control belt, slowly raised a burnished arm. A massive discharge of energy leaped from his accusing finger across to the already devastated Kosnaks. The parade ground before them disappeared in a haze of flame.

*

Tolemy, no longer protected by the warrior maiden, was making his way, alone, across the airfield when the explosions began. By the time he reached the square it was all over and Bob and Leslie were doing their best to comfort and reassure their fellow humans.

'Good God!' roared General Spiby, catching sight of his blazered rescuer. 'It's that man from the Building Society!'

Tolemy wandered amongst the smouldering Kosnak guards. He was drawn to a figure lying to one side of the carnage. For a moment he glimpsed the plastic likeness of his old friend Professor Melmo. Then the plasmic shield melted like a snowman in the sun, revealing the stark and twisted core of the robot they had originally created at Tinkerbell Toys.

'Where's Marcia?' said Drumnadrockit joining the boy.

'Out of action, I'm afraid,' said Tolemy. But before he could explain further there was a roar of turboprop engines on the far side of the airfield.

'Those robots have taken my plane!' cried Flight-Lieutenant Glaister.

CHAPTER NINE

Justin Watkin stared, bleary-eyed, at the two young women. 'I understand from the Head of Special Branch that you have some important information?'

Eddie and Hodge looked tired and drawn. They had dashed to London - despite the lateness of the hour - as soon as Inspector Cordingly telephoned from Tregolls, in an attempt to explain the situation directly to the minister. 'The robots, built by the man you call Professor Melmo, are about to attack the world.' Hodge put the matter in a nutshell.

The minister looked down at the cuffs of his pink pyjamas which shot from under the sleeves of the green Barber he had borrowed from his wife. 'Perhaps we should have a word with the professor about that, or the Head of Research.' He spoke slowly, trying not to show his irritation at being woken and called into the office on what was obviously an elaborate practical joke.

'Melmo's just another robot!' interrupted Eddie, remembering her fruitless visit to Henry Fraddon. 'And Bidmead is dead!'

The minister now decided it was all a dream. Shortly he would wake up, safe and sound, in his little house in Eaton Mews.

Henry Fraddon hurried into the room, swathed in a large turquoise skiing jacket. 'You've heard the news?'

'You mean it *isn't* a dream?'

'Of course it's not a dream. Your precious robots have gone and wiped out RAF Tregolls!' Fraddon, with the project turned sour, was swift to distance himself from the entire android enterprise.

'*My* robots?'

'They are almost certainly heading for London,' added Hodge. 'Their attack will be timed to coincide with today's meeting of world leaders.'

The phone rang on the minister's desk. 'Yes?' said Fraddon briskly. He turned to Justin Watkin who was rubbing his eyes in disbelief. 'General Spiby is on his way back to Northolt. Traffic Control are putting you through.'

General Spiby sat on the jump seat in the cramped flight deck of the reconnaissance aircraft they had commandeered from the Cornish airbase. In front of him, on the left, Three was flying the plane like an expert. (Flight-Lieutenant Glaister, who had never converted to jets, was relegated to the co-pilot's seat). The robot throttled back the engines of the old Comet and they began their descent to London Northolt.

'Of course we can't track them!' Spiby shouted into the radio telephone. 'They have sophisticated anti-radar devices.'

'I don't see what I can do about it,' came the plaintive voice of the distant minister.

'Cancel the conference, for a start,' bawled General Spiby over the roar of the slipstream round the landing gear.

'Out of the question,' protested Justin Watkin through the R/T. 'The summit begins in four hours' time!'

'Then we will have to isolate the whole of central London.' The general disconnected his headset and scrambled through into the main cabin. 'Politicians!' he growled.

'They're the same the Universe over.' Drumnadrockit looked up from where he was examining the lifeless body of the metal lady which they had salvaged from the tarmac of RAF Tregolls. 'If it wasn't for politicians the Vardon race would never have been destroyed.'

'Nor would the Kosnaks,' added Bob. He glanced at his watch. 'They must have landed by now.'

'But *where*?' said Tolemy.

'There are plenty of unmanned airfields round London

with enough runway for an Andover,' replied the RAF orderly.

Inspector Cordingly peered down at the lights of West London. 'Let's hope to God we're ready for them!' he observed grimly.

By breakfast time the whole of Trafalgar Square was filled with army lorries.

Mrs James read all about the elaborate security precautions for the summit meeting in her copy of the *Mail On Sunday*. She looked up from the kitchen table in Beachcroft Close. 'Tell Tolemy his egg's getting cold.'

'I'll have it,' said Terry James. 'Tolemy's up and out.'

'With Eddie Fox?' said Mrs James doubtfully, searching for the feature on wife-swapping in Torquay.

Mr Fox heard the news on the radio while he was shaving. 'A mile-wide security cordon has been drawn around Lancaster House where the talks are due to begin about now,' said the BBC announcer.

'Don't forget we're having drinks this morning with the Attwoods,' Bernard Fox shouted to his wife.

'Is Edwina invited?'

'She's already out. Doubtless off to see young Tolemy,' said Mr Fox with unaccustomed asperity.

'I declare this conference open,' said the British Prime Minister in the old ballroom of Lancaster House, hoping not to be questioned about the unusual security arrangements.

'Those unspeakable things will never get past the SAS,' announced General Spiby, perched on his shooting stick beside the Mobile HQ in Horse Guards Parade.

'I hope you're right,' said Tolemy, sitting with Eddie Fox on the steps of the military bus that had brought the Vardon robots from Northolt airfield.

'They'll only attack somewhere else,' said Eddie gloomily.

'Don't worry.' Inspector Cordingly stepped from the control van. 'All Police Divisions in the UK are on full alert.'

'It'll be here. I *know* it,' said Tolemy, starting to feel unnerved by the slow, quiet waiting.

'Good,' said the general who had become as disillusioned as Henry Fraddon with his treacherous knights. 'We can blow the lot of them to kingdom come!'

And so the day passed. Across the Mall from Horse Guards Parade, in an elegant, eighteenth-century mansion, the world leaders discussed the bomb, aid to the Third World and economic revival. In Beachcroft Close Terry James dug the garden while Mrs James roasted a small shoulder of lamb. In Turlow Old Town the Foxes talked about the new GCSE syllabus over Cyprus sherry and Twiglets with Pip and Jane Attwood; and the Attwoods told Bernard and Jasmine Fox about their holiday in Lanzarotte. In Oxford Circus and Leicester Square, on Waterloo and Westminster Bridge, at the end of the Strand, in Piccadilly and Hyde Park, an impenetrable ring of armed soldiers waited for an attack by alien machines.

'Nothing's going to happen,' said Charity O'Toole who had walked across the Mall from the press room in Lancaster House.

'False alarm,' agreed Justin Watkin who was discussing the situation with General Spiby. 'Damned shame we went and cancelled that tattoo.'

'Ms O'Toole peered inside the windows of the airforce bus. 'Perhaps the President could see some of *these* robots in action?'

'He'll see some action all right,' said Tolemy ominously.

Inspector Cordingly came running from the HQ with a police computer print-out in his hand. 'The empty clothes of a missing train driver have been found beside the track – at Cockfosters Underground Station!'

There had been no trains on the Piccadilly Line through Leicester Square for over half an hour. Frustrated passengers crowded the underground platform.

'Typical Sunday service!' muttered an off-duty ward sister from St John's Hospital, already late for lunch with her parents at Osterley Park.

There was a rattle in the gloom of the tunnel. A dozen Germans en route for Heathrow elbowed their way ruthlessly forward. The unfortunate tourists came face to face with eight hideous, black, insect shapes that burst from the darkness.

'Kosnaks supreme! Vardons destroyed!' screeched the cyber creatures.

In Horse Guards Parade, Inspector Cordingly and Tolemy stared at each other in horror. The enemy were already inside the security ring without a single shot being fired. 'They've come down the tube tunnels!' cried Tolemy.

There was a terrifying cry from the direction of Piccadilly as three fierce Kosnaks emerged from the booking hall of Green Park Station sending a party of Italian tourists screaming for shelter in the foyer of the Ritz. The leading Kosnak let loose an ordnance canister which shook the hotel to its foundations.

'Blimey!' An army sergeant, alerted by radio, came running with six of his men out of Half Moon Street. He stared for a second at the abominable creatures. 'Take cover!' The soldiers leapt behind an abandoned taxi a millisecond before the Kosnaks let loose a devatasting laser barrage.

There was a roar as the Section Commander fired his bazooka. A single robot fell writhing to the ground with an ear-splitting shriek. The remaining two Kosnaks retaliated with a power bolt discharge which wrecked the Jack Barclay Rolls Royce Showrooms.

At Hyde Park station more cyber insects erupted from the west-bound line. The passengers who could not make it to the escalators were the lucky ones as the Kosnak surrogates sythed their way upwards to the station entrance.

Three SAS men lay smouldering on the pavement outside the offices of Olympic Airways. 'Regroup!' shouted the sergeant.

As the soldiers retreated into Green Park two Kosnaks lumbered after them, advancing inexorably in the direction of Lancaster House. A hail of rapid rifle fire rained on the alien machines - to no effect whatsoever.

'There's another of the blighters!' The sergeant pointed to a four-legged device which came lolloping across the park behind them.

'Have no fear. I am your friend,' cried Mog. He crouched on his hind legs and a tongue of dragon's fire burst from his mouth. The two Kosnaks were surrounded by searing flame. One of the robots spun round and split apart, components spilling like blood and guts in all directions. But, as the smoke cleared, a surviving alien could be seen diverting towards Piccadilly circus.

The radio links to the Control HQ were redhot with news of similar attacks. Kosnaks were erupting from the underground railway tunnels at Victoria, St James, Westminster and Hyde Park.

'Take cover! Take cover!' screeched Three, darting across the roundabout at the bottom of Park Lane.

The Sunday strollers supposed the weird octopoid to be the property of some ingenious model maker, bound for Kensington Gardens - until they caught sight of the policemen in riot gear taking up their positions along the road. An armour-plated police bus (now fortunately empty) dissolved in a miasma of white as a contingent of Kosnaks materialised from the Underground.

'Use your laser blasters!' cried Three.

As more of the cyber-creatures poured from the Piccadilly Line the men of the riot squad fumbled with their alien weapons (conveniently provided by Tinkerbell Toys). Four leading Kosnaks burst apart in the ensuing fire-fight; but still more metal insects swarmed from their subterranean nest.

'There is no cause for alarm,' said the voice on the BBC. 'Military exercises are currently taking place in Central London. We repeat. There is no cause for alarm...'

In the conference room at Lancaster House the delegates listened nervously to the sounds of battle. 'Just a routine security exercise,' said the British Prime Minister, fingers crossed under the green baize table. 'We don't have revolutions in England.' The PM smiled at the President of the French Republic.

Tolemy, Bob, Hodge and Lesley Hastie cowered together in the bus, together with the lady from the USA. 'Don't think much of this for a game of soldiers,' said Bob.

'We must *do* something to help!' said Tolemy grabbing an electro-bombard and a handful of spare anti-robotic devices which he stashed in Mr Hastie's haversack.

'Are you out of your mind!' said a shivering bundle on the back seat.

'Come on!' said Tolemy, throwing a lazooka at the terrified Charity O'Toole.

St Martin's Lane was deserted as thirteen Kosnak warriors advanced from Leicester Square in the general direction of Lancaster House to the south. They quickly joined forces with another hit squad of armed robots who had come down Long Acre from the tube station at Covent Garden (causing pandemonium amongst the tourists in the piazza and several heart attacks to elderly members of the Garrick Club who were watching from the windows of the upstairs bar).

A young platoon commander came running round the post office in William IV Street. For a moment he stood spellbound at the sight of the Kosnak forces ahead. 'Give those tin bastards all you've got!' he yelled at his men. Instantly, flickering tongues of deadly laser fire leapt up the street, exploding three Kosnaks and hurling four others squirming with malfunction to the ground. 'Forward!' ordered the platoon commander, intoxicated with the power of his new weaponry.

A hail of energy bolts, discharged by the surviving Kosnaks, dissolved three of the soldiers in the gutter just outside the Pizza Hut and sent the others running for cover in the doorway of the Coliseum.

Mr Yasimoku, a visitor from Tokyo, was standing with his family and several Nikons in the centre of Piccadilly Circus, admiring the statue of Eros as a contingent of cyber-insects advanced from Regent Street. Mistaking the marching robots for an updated version of the Changing Of The Guard, Mr Yasimoku raised his Nikon – only to find the machine atomised by a devastating ray from another mechanism (and of far greater power than anything out of Japan). Chortling with terror, the Yasimokus took refuge behind the monument, only to find another division of automata goose-stepping forward from Shaftsbury Avenue.

'What the hell do you think you're doing!' shouted a sergeant lying beside the steps of Nelson's Column as Tolemy and his friends ran into Trafalgar Square from

Admiralty Arch. The soldier took a quick pot shot at a Kosnak as it tried to exit from the tube steps on the corner of the Strand.

'Get down, Tolemy!' shouted Bob Love, pushing the boy to one side. A Kosnak power bolt whistled over their shoulders, amputating the tail of a Landseer Lion.

'I'm an expert on robots,' said Tolemy, now prone on the paving stones beside the sergeant.

From the foyer of the English National Opera, the platoon Commander nervously eyed the line of Kosnaks striding relentlessly towards them down St Martin's Lane. 'Wait till they're closer,' he whispered to his men.

'Look, sir!' shouted one of the soldiers.

The officer turned. Another swarm of cyber-insects had split from an attack cluster in Charing Cross road and had turned back to reinforce their fellow robots in St Martin's Lane. The soldiers were trapped between the two converging forces.

Drumnadrockit stood beside the National Portrait Gallery, his psycho-sensors whirring. He took a round object from his belt and flung it high into the air. The alien artifact hovered, spinning like a catherine wheel above the beleaguered soldiers. Miniaturised magnetic grenades rained down from the device, each targeting a Kosnak warrior. The platoon commander and his men stared in amazement as the besieging robots exploded around them like giant firecrackers.

'We seem to be holding our own,' announced General Spiby at the Horseguards Parade HQ. But, even as he spoke, a dozen Kosnaks could be seen approaching the Victoria Memorial from the direction of Buckingham Gate. The leaders of the western world were virtually within the aliens' sights.

With a blood-curdling scream, Osmoses, who had been gunning down Kosnaks, one by one, as they attempted to descend from Lower Regent Street by the Duke of York Steps, charged straight down the centre of the Mall. As he drew level with the entrance of Clarence House he hurled a percussion canister at the advancing robots. There was an electrifying flash and the cyber-creatures were reduced to puddles of molten metal. (As were the railings of

Buckingham Palace). 'Howzat!' yelled Os.

'Thank God the Queen's at Windsor for the weekend,' murmured General Spiby.

Beside him in the van an SAS officer gave a bellow of triumph. 'Fifteen enemy robots destroyed outside Marks & Spencers in Oxford Street!'

'Thirty Kosnaks surrounded in Piccadilly Circus,' said Inspector Cordingly, beginning to look quite optimistic.

But the news was not all good. 'Major Libby reports a massing of enemy troops in Pall Mall,' said a grim-faced ADC.

'Who are *you*?' said a fat, pompous officer as Tolemy and Hodge ran to join the depleted army unit at the head of Cockspur Street.

'Tolemy James,' said Tolemy.

'Soon to be a very dead Tolemy James,' said Major Libby, his double chin puckering with fear. 'Those things are mustering for a final attack.'

'Not if I can help it,' said Tolemy, taking a couple of silver boxes from Mr Hastie's haversack. 'If we can generate a quantum effect from these programme scramblers . . .' he threw one of the units to Hodge and peered across the massing Kosnaks to where Mr Hastie and Charity O'Toole should already be in position on the corner of Waterloo Place. 'Now!' shouted the boy through Major Libby's loudhailer.

There was a waspish buzzing from the metal contingent in front of them. The robots jerked and gyrated, but were incapable of co-ordinated movement.

'Fire!' shouted the major, whereupon the soldiers let rip with lasers, paralysers, blasters and bombards at the helpless Kosnaks.

'Geronimo!' screamed Charity O'Toole further down Pall Mall, the lazooka in her hand spending like a fire hose.

'I say, well done, Tolemy,' grunted Major Libby as he stepped forward to examine the smouldering ironmongery.

Two metal creatures stood alone in a tiny alley. 'Za tonta Earth mikon, Tolemy,' announced one of the Kosnaks, scanning the humans in the wide street ahead.

'Zak mikon, Tolemy, puzan rosmor Kosnaka,' recorded his companion dispassionately, raising a jagged arm with which to moleculise the Earth Child who had destroyed so many of his fellow robots.

Tolemy saw a sudden movement in the shadows. He knew, at once, that there was no time to take cover.

There was a sudden, savage mewling from behind the boy as Mog leapt forward, fire already spitting from his mouth. An explosion followed immediately in the entrance to the alleyway.

'Thanks, Mog,' said Tolemy, grateful to find himself still alive.

'Don't mention it,' said the supercat with an attempt at modesty which fooled no-one.

The radio crackled as Major Libby communicated with HQ. 'The battle seems to be over,' he declared, a complacent smile on his face as if he had masterminded the entire action himself.

Listen!' said Tolemy.

A low-flying aircraft came roaring over Admiralty Arch.

It's the Andover!' cried Mr Hastie.

Suddenly the sky above them was full of dark-green, drifting shapes.

They've parachuted in a second wave,' said Spiby in dismay as the cyber-insects floated down towards the conference building.

The Leaders of the Free World had just concluded their meeting with a joint agreement on international terrorism when four Kosnak parachutists burst into the chamber like hijackers on a Pan Am 747. Kosnaks supreme! Vardons destroyed!' cried the leading robot, the one who had dubbed himself Modred at King Arthur's castle.

The rulers of Earth gazed in fear and wonder at the revolting automata.

'Power! Domination! Control!' screamed the Kosnaks, their sharp, claw-like arms raised in a brutal salute.

'You!' The Kosnak leader stabbed a jagged finger at the American President. Two of the robots moved forward and escorted their august and terrified hostage out of the room.

Outside, the soldiers, who had successfully dealt with the first wave of Kosnaks, were closing in on Lancaster House.
'We should attack immediately!' cried Spiby.

'No,' said Tolemy. 'They'd only kill all the politicians.'

The general wondered, for a fleeting moment, if that wouldn't be rather a good thing.

'We must wait and see if my plan works. It's our only hope.'

There was a smile on the presidential face as the hostage returned to his fellow delegates.

'Are you all right?' whispered the German Prime Minister, surprised to see the American leader back so soon.

'Well, you guys. I've had a talk with our Kosnak friends, and I'm here to tell you we've got a pretty good deal.' His fellow statesmen stared at him in amazement. 'Robots are nothing to be afraid of. With their help we can make the world a better place.' He suddenly whipped a silver box from his pocket. 'Move your arses!' he yelled. 'All of you!'

The subsequent rush of Top People to the doors was like the January Sales at Harrods. The warlike Kosnaks, meanwhile, were stiff as statues under the influence of the radiation from the box.

With an enormous crash a rather sooty Three landed in the grate of the ornate fireplace. A laser barrel extended in each hand, he blazed at the immobilised Kosnak robots. Each and every cyber-fascist burst apart like a ruptured appendix.

'It worked!' shouted Tolemy as he walked with General Spiby up the grand staircase, while ahead of them, Drumnadrockit and Osmoses picked off the remaining invaders.

'What exactly did you do?' said the general, confused.

'I put Marcia's matrix in the dummy of the President. When it was activated it behaved just like a Vardon.'

'Well done, old chap!' The general put an arm round the boy's shoulders.

On the landing, behind a marble bust of the Emperor Hadrian, something moved. The circuitry of a Kosnak survivor had organically reformatted to jam the debilitating signal from the silver box. The revitalised robot strode forward to the top of the stairs and raised a supercharged annihilator at the approaching teenager.

'Tolemy, get down!' screamed Mog from the hall below.

General Spiby pushed the boy away from him, raised his

service revolver, and fired.

Across the landing, Osmoses hurled a spinning disc at the Kosnak. The hostile robot erupted in a mushroom cloud of purple steam.

Tolemy opened his eyes, uncurled himself and stood up. 'General Spiby?'

Beside the boy was a crumpled officer's uniform, a swagger stick and a smoking gun.

The President of the USA stared down at his Kosnak double, wondering what would have happened to the world if they had swopped places as the aliens intended. It was certainly a remarkable likeness, although the prosthetic flesh of the dummy was now twisted and scarred by the cross-fire. The robotic brain had already been removed and was in the process of being restored to its rightful owner.

'Well done, Tin Lizzy,' said Tolemy, sliding the matrix into the handbag of the de-energised torso which had been brought in from the bus.

'My name is Marcia!' said the robot severely, as it came to life.

'Have it your own way,' said Tolemy. 'It's just that Tin Lizzy is so much nicer.'

'I'll think about it,' said Her Ladyship graciously.

'Why, that sure is one fine hunk of woman!' declared the President as the Tin Lizzy got to her feet. The American leader turned to Charity O'Toole who had just come in with Justin Watkin and Henry Fraddon. 'We could use some of those friendly robots ourselves!'

'The Ferrous Five are all controlled by that boy,' said Charity O'Toole, pointing to Tolemy James.

Tolemy stared at the wrinkled, waxy face of the man who stepped forward to take his hand. Was it really the President, or just another super-transformer?

'Don't worry,' whispered Charity, guessing what was in the boy's mind. 'He always looks like that.'

Mrs James came into the lounge at Beachcroft Close with two plates of ham and lettuce. 'Anything on the telly, Terry?'

Mr James stared hypnotically at the screen which showed a view of Number Ten Downing Street where Eddie and Tolemy were shaking hands with the British Prime Minister. 'I think there's something wrong with the set,' said Mr James hoarsely.

'I dare say,' said his wife, her knife and fork frozen in mid-air.

'I'll ring Radio Rentals first thing in the morning,' said Terry James, reaching for the salad cream.

Bernard Fox was dead-heading the last of the roses in the back garden of *Westaways*. He decided it was a very good idea of Mr Attwood's to make Tolemy a prefect. The boy was getting a bit above himself and it would do him good to have some real responsibility.

Mr Fox ducked as a large helicopter roared over his head. 'Damned cheek!' He peered indignantly over the fence at the adjacent recreation ground where the chopper was settling on the grass. 'Get me my bird-watching glasses!' he shouted at his wife who had come to the back door to see what the noise was all about.

'Thanks for the lift,' said Tolemy to the tall man in the grey suit.

'Thank *you*,' said the President to Tolemy and Edwina as the pilot throttled up for the onward flight to Heathrow Airport.

'Well?' said Mrs Fox to her husband who seemed to be mesmerised by the view through his binoculars.

'It's too *much*!' cried Bernard Fox, throwing down the secateurs and hurrying to the house in search of a large Alka Seltzer.

'It's a long way to Tipperary,' sang Osmoses, bouncing up and down in the back of the van as they drove through the outskirts of Turlow New Town.

'Shut up, Os!' shouted Drumnadrockit, Tin Lizzy, Three and Mog in unison.

Tolemy and Eddie were waiting in the yard of Tinkerbell Toys as the Vardon robots scrambled from the pantechnicon, followed by Bob, Hodge and Leslie Hastie.

'All's well that ends well,' said Drumnadrockit as they

trooped into the portacabin office.

'What happens now?' said Tolemy, staring at the battle-scarred Five and suddenly feeling very tired.

'We dismantle the robots,' said Bob Love ruthlessly.

The resulting din of protest could be heard on the other side of town.

'What do we want with a private army?'

'Five of us is hardly an army,' said Tin Lizzy pedantically.

'Bugger me!' cried Hodge. 'We can't throw away all that technical knowledge.'

'I agree,' said Leslie Hastie who planned – with a little help from Drumnadrockit – to write the definitive account of ley lines in Britain.

'They've brought us nothing but trouble,' continued the works manager lugubriously. 'We've got rid of one lot. Let's scrap these while the going's good.'

'The Kosnaks may be finished,' said Drumnadrockit. 'But you're still going to need our help. Your world is such a dangerous place!'

'There really *is* no alternative,' declared the Iron Lady.

'Don't put me to sleep,' pleaded Mog.

'I should cocoa!' shouted Os.

'You never know when I'll come in handy,' whispered Three, not to be outdone.

'Of course, it's up to you, Tolemy,' said the senior robot.

Osmoses, Mog, Three, Tin Lizzy and Drumnadrockit all looked at Tolemy James. So did Hodge and Bob and Mr Hastie.

Tolemy thought about his conversations with the Man in Black. He heard, in his head, the voice of Professor Melmo. *Power and knowledge can be used in so many ways.* How he wished his old friend were there to help him.

'Well?' said Drumnadrockit.

'I wonder!' said Tolemy.

EPILOGUE

A stiff, grey figure marched resolutely down Whitehall.

'Good God!' cried Henry Fraddon, passing the late arrival in the doorway of the Annex. 'Arthur Spiby! They told me you copped it in Lancaster House.'

'Old soldiers never die.'

'My dear fellow, I'm so pleased for you. Come along to the club and I'll treat you to a very large whisky.'

The military man backed nervously into the gloomy office building. 'There is much work to be done,' he muttered gruffly. 'And I never - ever - drink. Goodnight to you, Fraddon.'

It was only the beginning.